CLARENCE BUDINGTON KELLAND

Where There's Smoke

HARPER & BROTHERS   PUBLISHERS   NEW YORK

This book was published originally in *The Saturday Evening Post*
under the title of *Arson, Incorporated.*

Kelland, Clarence Budington, 1881–
    Where there's smoke. New York, Harper ₁1959, °1958₁

    186 p.   22 cm.

    "Published originally in the Saturday evening post, under the title
of Arson, incorporated."

    I. Title.

PZ3.K28Wh   813.52   59–6336 ‡

Library of Congress

Where There's Smoke

CHAPTER ONE

CRAIG BATTS, uniform coat removed in the heat of the morning, sat at the housewatch desk. His tour of duty on that post was from nine o'clock in the morning until noon, and his duties, while not arduous, were exacting and precise. He must record all fire alarms on the blackboard on the wall at his left and enter all important events in the record book opened before him. He must receive visitors with affability and courtesy. He must see to it that the street in front of the engine house was kept free of traffic so that the swift exit of the apparatus on its way to answer an alarm would not be impeded—and he must firmly prevent unaccompanied females from invading the premises.

Craig was one of the eleven thousand, six hundred and thirty-six uniformed firemen scientifically trained to prevent or to extinguish fires in the metropolis of Greater New York. Physically he was fit, twenty-six years of age, five feet, eleven inches tall, weight a hundred and seventy-six pounds. He was toughly handsome. He had the chin and neck and deep-set eyes of a light heavyweight pugilist. To look at him as he sat or walked with springy step, you would have thought that he ran more to muscle than brain and that he would be more adept at muscular activity than mental adroitness. You would have been in error. Not only was he a young man who could tell the difference between a syllogism and a solecism, but inside his well-shaped skull was a brain that could do odd tricks and perform feats that flabbergasted the beholder. Craig had had a natural bent that way which he had cultivated with assiduity in his spare time, in the belief that it might someday come in handy.

1

He had been a contented member of the fire department for nearly five years.

Behind him as he sat facing the street was a pumper with its hundreds of feet of folded hose and a cumbersome ladder and water tower, the latter threatened with obsolescence by improvements in method. In the corner was the spacious ambulance—an ambulatory hospital with multiple cots, and so roomy and completely equipped that a surgeon could perform a major operation in case of necessity.

At the rear of the building was an oblong room housing a long table on which meals were served, and to the left a kitchen where they could be prepared. Upstairs were dormitory and offices.

Craig, not disturbed by alarms of fire or by visitors, played with his trick mind, passing away the time with it as if it were an instructive toy. He would peer at a pedestrian as he walked past the open front of the engine house. It required an average of twelve paces to traverse the distance in which the passer-by was visible. In that brief interval Craig memorized him—or her. Being young and lusty and in the vigor of youth, it was more fun to memorize *her* if she were comely and shapely than it was to memorize *him* if he were paunchy and shambling. Long ago, pursuant to this pastime, he had reached the saddening conclusion that a considerable majority of adult human beings had achieved a certain measure of repulsiveness, and that very few had managed to bear likeness to gods or goddesses—or Greek statues or Ziegfeld chorus girls.

He committed them to memory, and when they had passed out of his life he closed his eyes and recalled them with meticulous detail. He sought to remember every article of dress or adornment, each facial feature and line of figure, every mannerism or gesture or gait. As a result he could give so exact a description that there would be no difficulty in identifying the individual from his verbal portrait.

He would vary this by concentrating upon the whole street scene as visible from his seat, and then, with closed eyes, recalling it in all its variety of being, object, animal and movement. Because he sometimes amused himself by a display of his talent to his companions, he had earned from them the old police epithet of Camera Eye. In older days and perhaps today police departments stationed men with camera eyes in busy spots, especially in the financial

2

district, to scan the faces of passers-by and identify the features of persons of predatory proclivities who had been distinguished by having their photographs printed on handbills. A Camera Eye was a valued and pampered member of the force.

When not on housewatch duty Craig was tillerman on the ladder, which meant that he sat at the steering wheel which controlled the rear wheels of the long, cumbersome apparatus, and saw to it that the hind end followed the front end in a reasonable manner without peril to life, limb or property. A ladder steered like an automobile in front but like a ruddered boat behind. It was a job requiring strength, readiness, quick reflexes and no mean skill.

Craig had just been reciting to himself the various items which made up a not unprepossessing young woman with red hair when Fireman Lorch came out of the archway which led to the stairs and approached the desk.

"Report to Chief Fogarty," he said curtly. "I'll relieve you."

Craig mounted the stairs, turned to his left and entered an office facing the street. Inside were two desks back to back, their flat tops in order. On a board at the right was the strength of the Division consisting of four battalions, as, for example, the Sixth Battalion consisted of four engine companies and a ladder, while Battalion Eight varied this by adding a water tower.

A badger-gray fire fighter sat at the right-hand desk and he glowered upward at his junior with a menace which only the face of an Irishman long in authority could exhibit.

"Orders is," he said deep in his throat, "for-r ye to rayport for-r-rthwith to the Chief Fire Marshal."

"Yes, sir," Craig answered respectfully.

"Ye did pr-r-oper," growled the Chief, "when ye come to me and asked per-r-mission to make your application to the Commissioner. For-r your transfer."

"Yes, sir," Craig said a second time.

The eyes of the Chief were the eyes of a disgruntled henhawk. "The old-time uniformed r-ranks was good enough for-r me," said the Chief. "It was plenty good for your fayther, and for-r manny thousands of staunch and worthy min."

Craig's eyes danced as he answered. "The old-time religion," he intoned, "was good enough for me. It was good for my mither, it was good for my fayther. . . ."

"Don't deave us wit' your crackin' wise and kape a rayspectful tongue in your head." He leaned forward suspiciously. "Was thim not the worrds of a Protestant hymn? What are we comin' to! A lad that was altar boy in St. Aloysius' singing a Protestant song." He scowled at Craig for seconds, but the young man did not flinch. "We will now," he said, "cease to be official. Why the divil do ye crave to be a fire marshal and desert the uniformed ranks? Tell me that."

"Uncle Paddy," Craig said earnestly, "it's a job I think I'm cut out for."

"It's right ye may be," said the Chief grumpily. "As a lad ye was always pokin' and pryin' and stickin' your nose where it didn't belong. Always the curiosity of a cat in a strange house. Maybe 'twill be for the best to make yer snoopin' legal instead of a troublesome nuisance. . . . I'm not sayin' a marshal can't be a credit to the department. . . . So go your ways, thin. Are ye off or on this night?"

"Off, Uncle Paddy."

"Then," said the old officer, "you will rayport for supper at the house at sivin by the clock and tell me how ye make out and what the Chief Marshal had to say to ye whatever."

"Yes, sir," Craig said, resuming formality and snapping a salute.

Chief Fogarty was no blood uncle to Craig Batts, but only a generation-long crony of that old smoke-eater, Deputy Chief Batts, who had been Craig's father until he lost his life in an action far above and beyond the call of duty in the great tenement fire of six years ago. Having no son of his own but only a daughter, Chief Fogarty had placed himself *in loco parentis* to Craig. Indeed he had brought him up almost as his own son and had not spared the rod. Between the two men, young and old, was deep affection, and on the part of the younger an all but reverent respect.

Craig rode the subway downtown to the Municipal Building, and the elevator carried him upward to the floor where were the offices of the high executive brass of the fire department. He gave his name and mission at the information desk and was directed to the office of the Chief Fire Marshal. The Marshal's aide looked up from his desk.

"Fireman Batts?" he asked.

"Yes, sir."

"Go in. The Marshal will see you."

4

Craig opened the door and entered a roomy office, at the window end of which was a spacious flat-top desk with telephones and papers. On a cabinet at the right a box spoke intermittently. The man at the desk cocked his ear. "Search proceeding for radioactive material in school building," the voice squawked, and electricity crackled. The Chief Marshal, not stiff with dignity, cast information to Craig. "Alarm of radioactive stuff in a public school. They're searching." He snorted. "What have they got, a boy with radioactive britches?"

The Chief Marshal was a broad man, not in uniform, not tall but bulky, with round, genial face, whose amiability could swiftly become something quite different. Those steel-gray eyes told their story. He fixed his eyes upon young Craig.

"Your name again," he said.

"Fireman Craig Batts, sir."

The Chief Marshal tapped a paper on his desk. "The Commissioner," he said, "forwarded your application for transfer to my department." He narrowed his eyes and squinted searchingly up at Craig. "What makes you think you have the makings of a fire marshal?"

"I believe, sir, I have definite qualifications."

"Do you say so now?" Craig could not determine if the Chief Marshal was being ironic. "Suppose you enumerate them."

"I notice things, sir. I remember details. I am able to draw conclusions from what I see."

"A modest lad," said the Chief Marshal sourly.

"Sir," replied Craig, "you asked a question. I replied to it honestly."

"Not hiding your light under a bushel."

"Sir," said Craig, "to become a fire marshal is a thing I desire greatly. I am here to convince you of my fitness for the place. I am not vain, sir, nor do I brag. But it would not be good sense to belittle myself."

A snort was the answer to this. "So you observe and notice details and make deductions. Those things a competent marshal must do. He must do it not where everything is cozy, but in lofts or cellars where he is being roasted by flames or choked by smoke or the reek of acid fumes. It is in such conditions that a marshal must observe and remember and deduce. . . . And keep alive."

5

"Yes, sir," Craig said.

"We have no artificial way to create such conditions," said the Chief Marshal. "A man must prove himself in actual practice."

"But, sir, might I respectfully suggest that I might prove what I have said? If you will make a test."

"Young man," said the Chief Marshal, "this service has its traditions and its history and its pride. There is a plaque of your father in the fire college out in Long Island City."

"I expect no special favors," Craig said a bit stiffly.

"You will get none," snapped the Chief Marshal. Then he smiled and it was a sly and boyish smile. "But neither will there be prejudice against you. I'm a busy man, but what is your test?"

"If I may make so bold, sir. Will you do this? While I turn my back will you place a number of things on your desk? Little articles."

"How many?"

Craig shrugged. "Suit yourself, sir. . . . I will turn my back. Then at your signal I will face the desk and concentrate upon the objects while you tick off ten seconds. Then I turn my back again. I will try to name the several articles, state their use and make deductions from the fact that you had them in your pockets."

"Ten seconds, you say."

"Yes, sir."

"Right. Turn around."

Craig turned. He heard movement, clinkings, rustlings, slithering. He experienced elation and confidence in himself. This was the sort of test he had neither anticipated nor hoped for, but at last it would give him opportunity to put his trick mind to some valid purpose. Maybe this was the crucial moment for which he had been training himself.

"Now turn," said the Marshal. He counted ten slowly, and once more Craig presented his back.

"All right," said the Marshal with an ominous note in his throaty voice. "Let's see you do your stuff."

Craig stood silent and relaxed, head bent so that his chin touched his chest, eyes closed.

"Well. Well," said the Chief impatiently.

"Yes, sir," Craig responded. He would make a production of it to impress. It must not seem easy. "There are," he said, "eleven

6

articles. Five in a straight line and six scrambled. In the line beginning at your right is a knife, its handle of polished steel. It contains a large blade, a small blade, a nail file, a corkscrew, a screwdriver, a small pair of scissors and a bottle opener. Next is a small silver box about an inch long and three-quarters of an inch wide, with a design on top of crossed arrows and zigzag lines probably representing lightning flashes. The third thing is a menthol inhaler. Next to it is a yellow wooden golf tee, and last a gold bill clip ornamented by a wee gold coin. There used to be tiny gold dollars. I couldn't see its date."

He mopped his forehead and exhaled and tensed his shoulders as if under severe strain.

"Go ahead. Six to go," said the Chief Marshal.

"First I remember a small brass swivel with a ring on each end. Next a bit of a metal thing. Some sort of key." The Chief could see the cords in Craig's neck swell as with the effort of concentration. "Oh, yes, an old watch key. Next an earring with the gadget that fastens it to the ear missing. After that a small red pencil about two inches long sharpened by a sharpener and not a knife. Number five is a folded piece of something like piecrust. . . ." He swallowed dryly. "It's one of those Chinese things with a slip of paper inside telling your fortune. And last," he said, hesitating again as if baffled and struggling to recall, "is a thing the like of which I never saw before. It is a gold cylinder with a ring on one end as if to hitch it to a watch chain. Not more than an eighth of an inch in diameter. Some kind of an antique. . . . I get it. Grandfather used to have one. A gold toothpick."

The Chief Marshal pursed his lips. He was impressed; indeed, he was astonished, but he was resolute not to let it show.

"All right, lad, turn around now. Not bad. Not bad for observation and remembering. Have ye the photographic eye? But now to use your brains. Small good to see and remember if you can't reason from there. What can you deduce from these trinkets?"

"The big knife, now," Craig said. "A sensible man like yourself would never buy such a clumsy, cumbersome thing. Yet you set store by it and carry it with you. A present." He closed his eyes and made a grimace. "Only a small boy would think such a thing a good present, because he would like to own it himself. I'd say your grandson."

The Chief uttered a gusty snort.

"The silver box is Indian make. Either you have visited Arizona or New Mexico, or it is a present from there. Either way it says you are a habitual pill-taker, probably a bit of a hypochondriac. Stomach trouble. The inhaler says you're subject to nose colds. You're a golfer and have played recently or you'd not have a tee in your pocket or a bit of a pencil to keep the score. The bill clip also is a present and a tasty one from a lady, a young lady of modern ways. Your daughter likely. Maybe the same whose earring you have there to take for her to the jeweler's to be mended."

"Proceed."

"You're a fisherman, the little brass swivel says. The watch key is to an old watch that you're proud of. I'd say it was a presentation watch to your father maybe. Was he too a fireman? And the toothpick was his as well. You take pride in your folks that have gone before you and you pamper your family, else a busy man like you would not be running errands for a daughter."

"That all?" the Chief asked disparagingly.

"Just general things like you're a pushover for your young ones. You even brought home for one of them that fortune thing from a Chinese restaurant where you ate the other night. And forgot about it. A man proud of your ancestors. You'd take delight to leave for your grandchildren an inscribed watch or a medal. . . . Is that enough, sir? It is exhausting."

The Chief Marshal returned the several articles to his pockets and his desk drawer. He pretended to listen to the voice coming out of the box. The alarm of radioactivity in the school was false. He drummed on his blotter without lifting his eyes to Craig's face.

"You come of a fire-fighting family," he said.

"Yes, sir."

"Why are you not content with the uniform branch?" he asked. "If you're ambitious, advancement can be quicker and you can rise higher. Over there you have thirteen hundred lieutenants. There are three hundred and sixty-eight captains and two hundred and twenty-nine battalion chiefs. Plenty of civil service examinations for promotion. Here in the Bureau of Fire Investigation we have only fifty-six persons. Of these twenty-one are civilian investigators and only nineteen from the uniformed force. Where, then, are the opportunities for promotion?"

8

"I still wish the transfer, sir."

"Is it the glamour of it? Is it that you want to play cops and robbers?"

Craig smiled and seemed very boyish. "I do want to play cops and robbers, sir," he said.

"There will be hard study."

"There is hard study in the uniformed branch."

"To be sure," the Chief Marshal admitted. "The department is changing. Under our commissioner the accent is on preventing fires, on educating the public. It's on inspections and patrols to minimize or eliminate fire risks. It's on educating people in their homes how to be careful, or in their shops or lofts. . . . Among other things you will have to learn bookkeeping and chemistry. And chemistry doesn't mean just knowing that H_2O is water. The city today is lousy with radioactive materials. Fifty years ago about all a fireman had to know was how to climb a ladder and squirt a hose. Now he's got to know how to cope with isotopes. Muscle and courage aren't enough. To rise in the department you must be a scientist."

"I've read about protons and electrons and neutrons," Craig said. "Since that fire in the electronics plant I've been digging in."

"It could be," said the Chief more to himself than to Craig, "that torches will be using atomic devices to touch off blazes instead of gasoline or phosphorus. For that day we must be ready." He snorted. "A man in Albany may be touching off a fire in the Bronx by remote control! . . . Before you can transfer to my department," he said directly to Craig, "there must be a vacancy. Return to your duty. If there comes a vacancy and I deem you fit to fill it, you will be notified."

"Thank you, sir," Craig said, and saluted and walked out of the office. When he was gone the Chief Marshal called in his aide from the outer room.

"John," he said, "there is a young man who must have his chance. I've seen his like but once. He's a natural. It's a trick mind he has, and if he doesn't get too big for his britches the day can well come when he'll bring pride to us all. If . . . If a trick mind isn't all there is to him. Could be he's nothing but a grown-up Quiz Kid."

"Not," said the aide, "if he takes after his father."

9

"I wonder," mused the Chief, "why he wants this transfer. The deep reason."

"I think I can make a guess," said the aide. "Do you recall that his father died in an incendiary fire—and that the torch was never caught?"

"Is it so? Is it so? That would be a moving reason, if he loved his father. We well know that getting even, revenge, is one of the prime motives of arson. Why, then, could it not be a strong reason for wanting to catch firebugs? . . . Anyhow I must have that boy and give him his chance."

CHAPTER TWO

THE FOGARTYS, father and daughter, occupied an apartment in Fortieth Street in Brooklyn. It was not a new apartment with all the modern gadgets, but no argument could move the Chief to up-root himself and find a residence in step with the march of progress. Being a conservative Irishman, than which nothing more conservative exists, he looked askance upon the novel and could not be convinced that A.D. 1958 was not a pawkish and decadent year as compared to 1914. With this his daughter of twenty summers and glorious red hair was in complete disagreement. Of course she had not experienced the serene and splendid days that came before the first World War. When the sun never set on the British flag—which naturally was anathema to her parent—and when you could always rent a dollar for six cents, and when the only contact a citizen had with his national government was when he went to the post office to buy a postage stamp. In the good old days, when her mother went to the beach she covered herself so completely and hideously as scarcely to be recognized as a human being. When Nora went to the beach she wore so little, and that so charmingly, that one could not mistake her as anything but one of the most desirable girls ever to dazzle the eyes of any male from sixteen to sixty-five. When first her father saw her in this regalia he bellowed so that the neighbors came running out, and was all for taking her across his knee and shutting her away in a dark closet. Which did not alarm her in the least.

For her father she kept house with skill and efficiency and a minimum of hard labor, for she imported into his kitchen every

11

labor-saving device from an electric dishwasher to a stove that sounded a tocsin when the roast was done. He roared about the expense of it and the nonsense of it and the evil ways of a girl afraid to put her hands in soap and water. To which she countered by asking why the department had swapped horses for gasoline motors and fitted its men with Scott Airpak respirators so that they could work in smoke- or reek-filled rooms for half an hour at a stretch instead of being dragged out to the hospital choking, gasping, maybe dying.

Her father came stomping up the stairs, for it was a walk-up apartment. From the door he bellowed, "Hey, Nora, set another place. There'll be company."

"Who?" she asked from the kitchen door.

"Young spriggins," he said, as if that were full and proper identification, which it was.

"You could have telephoned," she said severely.

"For why? So ye could cook something special? What's good enough for me is good enough for him."

"I'm not," she said, "thinking of quality but quantity."

"What's enough for two can always be stretched to three," he said didactically.

The bell rang and she ran to press the buzzer and open the door. Craig Batts was halfway up the stairs.

"The top of the evening to you, Cupcake," he called. He peered at her and shook his head disparagingly. "Your nose," he said, "is red as a rose."

"From sweating away my young life over a hot stove," she snapped. "And were you invited or did you crash the gate?"

"Don't be obstructing traffic. Out of a man's way."

She made as if to kick his ankle, but he sidestepped deftly and aimed a spank that missed.

"Oh, for a guest just once with manners," she said. "Who has time to say good evening before he makes for the icebox and a bottle of beer."

"Is the old man home?" he asked over his shoulder.

"He's washing behind his ears," Nora said. "A thing that would do you no harm."

He tossed his cap on the sofa and walked through to the kitchen where he helped himself to a bottle of beer. From his bedroom

12

Chief Fogarty could be heard in song, an Irish folk air of many verses. He emerged pink and scrubbed, still giving voice. But on the threshold he stopped, disgruntled that memory had failed him. "There's a hole in the ballad," he said, and fell silent while he strove to recall the words that would fill the gap.

He plumped himself down at the tastefully set and garnished table and uttered complaint to tease his daughter. "Time was, Craig," he said, "when a man could come home to comfort in his home. When he could kick off his shoes and eat hearty food in the kitchen."

"Time was," retorted Nora, "when the company ran up the hill pulling the hosecart by hand. You're a chief now, the highest any Fogarty ever climbed. So behave accordingly."

She placed before her father a platter of steak and a bowl of fluffy mashed potatoes. At her end of the table she set peas in cream and wee dishes to hold them, and a pot of coffee with cups and cream and sugar.

"What's special about this evening?" she asked. "What are you all swelled up with, Craig?"

"The boy was summoned by the Chief Fire Marshal," said Chief Fogarty. "To be put in his place, I hope, for wanting to leave the uniformed branch."

"You put in for a transfer to the Fire Marshal's department?" asked Nora critically. "Why?"

"Everybody asks me why," Craig complained.

She nodded her head in three staccato nods. "I know why," she said. "Did you make it?"

"Two," he said, "will get you ten I did."

Nora raised her brows and widened her blue eyes at her father. "Would you say he was too modest to get along?" she asked.

"Thinking ill of himself," said the Chief, "will never clog him from climbing the ladder."

"So," asked Nora, "you said to the Chief Marshal, and the Chief Marshal said to you—?"

"I did tricks for him," Craig said, "to the extent that I flabbergasted him."

" 'He stuck in his thumb,' " quoted Nora, " 'and he pulled out a plum, and he says What a Big Boy am I.' "

"What kept you so late at Eve Tourney's this afternoon?" he asked with an irritating grin.

"We were planning—" she commenced and then stopped, scowling at him. "All right. Show off. How did you know?"

"That you were late home is easy. You're a neat body, Nora, but your hat and gloves and bag were thrown anyhow on the seat in the hall. And you hadn't time to change your dress before you started supper. I know you didn't change your dress because there are a couple of white cat hairs on your skirt. And who has a white cat that always wants to jump on your lap?"

"The girl that marries you will be sorry for it," she said shortly. "With your spying eyes, she could have no secrets from you."

"A good wife," he said with counterfeit smugness, "should have no secrets from her husband."

"No girl can be a good wife unless she keeps many secrets from her husband," she retorted.

"Put a stop to your snapping back and forth," said the old Chief. "And tell me, Craig, what happened today."

Craig became serious. "I think it went well," he said.

"If he did not cast you out on your ear, then it went well," said Chief Fogarty. "He is not one to palaver. If you did not impress him well, he'd have given you short shrift."

As they finished the meal the buzzer sounded. Nora got up and went to the door and came back frowning.

"It's that man with the bristles again," she said. "Why does he come here with his good manners? And his cat's smile. What has he to do with you, Father?"

"Is it Mr. Tupper?" her father asked.

"It is him," Nora said without regard for grammar, which usually she held in respect. "I was of a mind to tell him you were not at home. But he walked right in. If I had not stepped aside, he would have trod on me."

"Is that so?" Craig asked, and flexed his shoulders. "Is he welcome in this house, Uncle Paddy?"

"It is a matter of business," the old man said, but neither face nor voice was happy, and his steel-gray eyes, usually so steady and level, shifted as if to avoid his daughter's gaze. "It is private business. You, Craig, will take Nora to the movies, or whatever."

"The dishes," Nora objected.

14

"You will leave the dishes," her father said in voice of command. And then with ill-simulated humor, "Twenty-three, skiddoo with ye."

"With his slang," Nora said, "Father is as up to date as a space ship. . . . If we are to be thrown out of our home for this imitation of a Fuller brush, let us be on our way."

They arose from the table and followed in the Chief's wake as he went into the sitting room. A man came to his feet as they entered, and Craig admitted the justice of Nora's description. Every hair on the man's head stood straight and erect, *en brosse*. Every hair was a needlelike bristle, and there were many of them, a bumper crop. This gave the handsome face a Prussian look, and definitely negated what otherwise would have been a feminine cast of countenance—or that of a feline. He was straight of back, with an exaggerated erectness as if it were a matter of pride with him to stand with shoulders back and chest outthrust. Craig estimated him. He would be a scant six feet in stature and he would weigh a hundred and ninety pounds. Craig had noted the easy grace of the man as he got to his feet, and how he stood balanced as if ready.

"My daughter you have met," said the Chief. "Our friend Mr. Batts, this is Mr. Tupper."

The men nodded curtly, each taking an instantaneous dislike to the other. Neither extended his hand.

"Charmed," said Mr. Tupper with irritatingly exaggerated courtesy. Craig contented himself with a nod.

"Miss Nora! More lovely than I remembered," Tupper said, bold eyes sweeping her from top to toe.

"From you," she said coldly, "I want no compliment."

The man raised his brows and spread his hands in a sort of comical dismay. "And how," he asked, not disconcerted, "may I have given offense?"

"I wish I knew," she said, more to herself than to him, and then walked past him and into the hall, very straight of back and little heels tapping the floor. Craig followed in her wake. She did not speak as they descended the stairs.

"A revolting man," she said, as they reached the sidewalk.

Craig halted and looked down at her. "Does he annoy you? Did he make a pass?" he asked softly.

"No. Always soapy good manners, except his eyes. X-ray eyes.

15

Why does he come? What's between him and Father? For days after he calls Father is not himself. He keeps silent. He avoids me. He acts—oh, it is a dreadful thing to say, but it's true. He acts as if he had been kicked."

"Shall I go back up and ask him questions?" Craig demanded.

Nora shook her head violently. "To do that," she said, "would wound Father's pride. He is a proud old man."

"By good right," Craig said, and meant it.

"Something is not right with him," Nora said, "but he must work it out himself."

"Could it be he's run into debt?"

"Father!" she exclaimed.

Nora was convincing. And Craig himself knew that, as the old saying has it, Chief Fogarty hated and feared debt as the devil hates holy water.

"If not money troubles, then what?" he asked.

"There's hardly a trouble," Nora said unhappily, "that, if you seek far enough, you don't find money at the root of it."

"He is a good man and a contented man and a wise man," Craig mused. "But there's nothing he would not do for you, Nora, and maybe for me. Or for someone he held in high respect and affection." He paused and frowned down at her. "Are you in any trouble, Nora?"

"No," she replied without rancor. "Are you?"

"No trouble," he answered. "That Tupper man has the air of a cat that's eaten the canary. . . . Look, Sugar Plum, the street is deserted, and I'd not be interrupted if I waited for him and knocked his teeth and the answer out of him at the same time."

"This is no time to be primitive," she said. "It is a time to be adroit."

"She makes," Craig said ironically, "with the college education."

"Also," she said, ignoring his remark, "if you're as noticing as you brag, you would have seen how his coat was loose but nevertheless that there was a bulge under his left arm."

"That I saw," Craig said, "and it did nothing to make me worry less. Why should your father be letting a gun-toting slicker set foot in his parlor?"

"It could be nothing to do with the department," she said

16

fiercely. "Next to his religion the department is the most sacred thing in his life."

"What we are afraid of, Cupcake, is that this Tupper is putting some sort of pressure on your father."

She nodded unhappily.

"Isn't it possible," he asked, "that the shoe is on the other foot? That your dad is tightening the screws on this man?"

"How could that be, Craig?" she asked, but with sudden hope surging upward and constricting her throat.

"Chief Fogarty," Craig said, "is a sharp old party. He's been around. He's had years of specialized experience. Maybe he's got wind of some skulduggery. . . ."

"It could be. . . . Oh, I hope that's the way it is. But his manner and Tupper's manner didn't indicate it was that way. And Father's an organization man, a member of a service. If he discovered something, was suspicious of something, would he try to run it down all by himself? I can't think so. If it touched the department, he'd report it—to the Commissioner, or to the Chief Fire Marshal."

They had been walking slowly as they talked so earnestly. Their snail's pace had not carried them to the corner, and there they paused uncertainly.

"Where to?" Craig asked. "Picture?"

"I'm in no mood for pictures," Nora said miserably.

"Somewhere to dance?"

She shrugged. "No," she said after a moment.

"Then how about going over to my place and watching television?"

She considered that suggestion. In neither of their minds was there even a faint thought of impropriety. It did not enter either of their heads that to go to his small apartment might be misconstrued by suspicious minds. Their relationship was more that of brother and sister than of boy and girl. "Yes," she said, "that would be nice. Just sit until it will be all right to go home."

They did not pay attention to a car parked at the curb—a car in which sat three young men smoking cigarettes and waiting. It called for no attention when the car started suddenly forward, reaching speed so quickly that a motor that had been worked upon by experts to give it extra speed was indicated. The sudden roar caused Craig and Nora to turn their heads and follow the sedan

17

with their eyes. They saw a man on the walk, turning toward them as if he had just emerged from the apartment house where the Fogartys lived. As the lurching car came abreast of the man there were two detonations not unlike backfires. But Craig saw an arm extended through the car's window and the flash of gunfire. The car sped away. The man on the walk had thrown himself flat upon the concrete of the sidewalk. For a moment it seemed that he had stopped a bullet. But he leaped to his feet, stood a moment staring after the vanishing car. He dusted himself off as best he could and then resumed his progress. He walked hurriedly toward Craig and Nora, and their startled eyes recognized him. It was the Mr. Tupper to whom they had been reluctantly introduced in Chief Fogarty's living room.

"Somebody," Craig said grimly, "doesn't like our Mr. Tupper."

CHAPTER THREE

THE PINGING of the 2-2-2 signal, most welcome of all sounds that assail the fireman's ear, announced that paychecks were on their way up from headquarters. This was so, just as the saddest of all signals to come over the air was the 5-5-5-5 announcing the death of a comrade.

Craig Batts, with four companions, were sitting at the rough table in the mess room adjoining the well-equipped kitchen at the left. They were at ease in shirtsleeves, enjoying a midmorning cup of scalding coffee. The morning papers had been read, the crossword puzzles completed and nobody seemed inclined to a game of cards.

"Doldrums," said Craig.

Jim Dodd, who was the statistical hound of the house, was moved to exhibit his specialty. "Always dullest from six in the morning till noon," he said. "Last year only 7,854 fires. Busiest time from noon till six, 21,531 fires."

"He ought to be on one of them question programs," jeered Ned Waters.

"Bet you a quarter," Craig said, "that he can tell you, within a hundred gallons, how much water we used last year to douse blazes."

"How could anybody know that, least of all the sloppiest buttman in the department?" A buttman is the fireman who braces the bottom end of a ladder when it is being raised by hand.

"Put up or shut up," Craig said genially.

Waters spun a quarter on the table and Craig matched it. "Speak your piece, Jim," he said.

"In 1955," Dodd said, preening himself, "we squirted 71,997,254 gallons of fresh water and 57,798,309 gallons of salt water."

Craig reached for his companion's two bits, but Waters protested. "How do I know he's right?"

"That's how it stands in the Commissioner's report," Dodd said. "I read it from cover to cover and I never forget a figure."

At that moment, over on Seventh Avenue, an excited citizen was turning in an alarm at Box 435. Miles to the north in the building of the Bureau of Fire Communications in Central Park a light flashed on one of the series of panels that formed an arc at the right of the desk of the Supervising Dispatcher, and in less than thirty seconds the alarm was automatically sent out over the transmitter to the zone affected. A first alarm.

The four men lounging at the table in the engine house resolved into action. Other firemen came sliding down the pole from the dormitory above. All leaped to their assigned stations, donning helmets and rubber coats and boots. Waters was chauffeur of the ladder, Craig was tillerman. Motors roared. The man on the housewatch desk hurried to the street to help clear it of traffic, and then leaped aboard the huge piece of apparatus as it screamed out of the house and swung left on the street. The smaller pumper followed. They waited for no man. Firemen must catch them on the run or be left behind.

Craig Batts, gripping the wheel that controlled the rear axle, must calculate to a nicety. Too much of a twist of his wheel would crash the juggernaut over the curb to collide with facing buildings, too little of a turn would cause disaster. Craig Batts experienced elation. The sensation of speed; the element of danger; the concentration required of him; the urgent warning sounds lifted his task far above drudgery and into the realm of excitement and contest. As he crouched over the tiller wheel, holding steady the stern of that huge vehicle, his were almost the sensations of a participant in some Olympic game, but played for higher stakes than the prizes in any footrace or decathlon. With iron grip he held the monster from swaying or wagging its tail as they turned southward and halted at the alarm box where an excited citizen motioned and shouted. But no directions were needed, for smoke was pouring

20

from the windows of a six-story brick warehouse, old, dingy, weather-beaten—a relic of an earlier generation.

As they stopped Craig and his chauffeur lifted down the thirty-five-foot ladder. This was routine. With Craig acting as buttman, they raised the ladder against the face of the building. The pumper had already reached its station and the Chief's red car. It was a first alarm to which four engines, two hook and ladders and one rescue unit had responded.

Already the Chief with his aide carrying a walkie-talkie had entered the building whose ground floor was free of smoke or gases. The creaking elevator was working but deserted. It carried them upward to the fourth floor, a dirty, cluttered loft, where, even in the murk, the Chief could note half a dozen violations of those rules laid down to minimize the risks of fire. Cartons were piled high so that they clogged the sprinkler system; the stairway upward was choked with rubbish; the rear windows through which light could scarcely penetrate were frozen shut. Over his walkie-talkie the Chief uttered curt orders. Outside the orders were obeyed. The water tower lifted its nozzle that could send a solid stream of water as high as the ninth story of any building. Connections were made with the stand pipe that ran up the face of the structure. Firemen using the stretch were lugging hose lines up the fire escape. Suddenly the Chief Fire Marshal made his appearance beside Chief Fogarty, his civilian clothes covered by a rubber coat, his feet in boots and a helmet on his head. The blaze had been in the right-hand corner, to the rear of the loft. As the Marshal arrived there was a second upsurge of flame over by the right-hand wall.

"Get a fog nozzle up here," he shouted to the Chief. "This one stinks."

Two wooden crates were burning stubbornly, and men who had at last succeeded in getting up a hose line directed its stream upon these cases. There was an immediate pyrotechnic display, silvery, blinding.

"My God," yelled the Chief, "keep water off those cases. Magnesium powder."

But it was too late. Water mingling with the magnesium liberated hydrogen gas, and there was a violent explosion followed by a choking cloud of smoke. The Chief and his aide and the Marshal

21

were hurled backward, shocked, choking, more than half unconscious. As they struggled to their knees, groping blindly, another fire came to life between them and the elevator shaft.

"Fog nozzle! . . . Fog nozzle! . . ." The Marshal half mumbled, half shouted, "Don't knock everything to hell with a solid stream. Don't destroy evidence."

"Yes, sir," responded a voice. It was Craig Batts, who, helping to operate the stretch, had hoisted hose up the rusty fire escape. At the end of the hose was not the ordinary nozzle to release a solid, powerful, destructive stream of water, but one that could be regulated as the nozzle of a garden hose is regulated to produce either a solid stream or a spray. Were there no other purpose for a fog stream than protection of advancing firemen it would be justified, for it interposes between the fire fighter and the blaze a screen of water which cools and smothers flame while it protects its operators from flame or smoke or gases. Behind this shield of water particles the men advanced, the fog washing and cooling the air as it moved forward, dispersing smoke and fumes, absorbing heat and almost miraculously extinguishing surface fires. Also, because it lacks volume and violence, it does not destroy evidence, if evidence exists, nor does it cause the water damage to perishables that must come from a solid stream hurling hundreds of gallons each minute.

Chief Fogarty and the Marshal, faces scorched, eyebrows and hair singed, coughing and gagging from inhaled smoke and reek, could well be hospital cases but they clung grimly to their place of duty. The Chief could only croak orders for his aide to transmit over the walkie-talkie. A second alarm went out over the air to be responded to by another hook and ladder and four engines. Now a Deputy Chief and Chief of Department would arrive to take over command.

The explosion had dispersed the fire through the rear of the loft, but reinforcements arrived, and a detachment from Rescue Unit Number Ten with a second fog nozzle. Solid streams smashed the frozen rear windows so that ventilation was established.

Everywhere in that choking atmosphere were speed, precision, accuracy, efficiency. Each man from Johnny-come-lately to Chief knew his place and his duty. The main thing now was to confine the fire, to prevent it from reaching up to the floor above or swooping down to the floor below. Men against a destructive element, and the intelligence of the men prevailed over the savagery of the most feared trilogy of earth, fire, water.

To a civilian, trapped in that loft, it would have seemed an inferno urging to panic; a dreadful holocaust from which there could be no escape. But to the men in helmets it was routine. Exciting routine; dangerous routine, but a ravening thing they knew how to handle. And they mastered it, drove it back, quelled it, until only embers remained, and air rapidly being purified by the fog. The fog nozzles did not abate their work until all danger of flashback was eliminated. Then, with one motion of the control device of the nozzle, the fog was changed to a solid stream to penetrate and extinguish any smoldering and deep-seated fire remaining.

Then the Chief Fire Marshal and his assistant took over, and systematic search for evidence of arson commenced. Craig, eyes smarting, throat burning, would have loved to remain and watch, but he was ordered elsewhere. Presently he was in the street performing the chores of lowering and replacing ladders, of returning hose to the pumpers, of preparing to return to the engine house which was his station. The apparatus lumbered back to its quarters, and, from each station which had been called to the fire, went to Communications Center in the Park the 4-4-4 signal informing that the unit is again "In Service" and ready to respond to another call.

As Craig mounted to his seat at the tiller he glanced up the face of the loft building; peered ahead and to either side, blinked burning eyes and was impatient to get back to where he could apply unguents to his minor burns. As he waited for the motor to roar to life he saw, pushing his way along the opposite sidewalk, a tall, vigorous figure in a beautifully tailored suit of blue serge. The man walked slowly, scowling, face turned toward the building in which fire had been extinguished. The man was angry. As Craig watched his face, struggling to identify him, the man spoke a curse and kicked viciously at a bit of rubbish on the walk. Even with watering eyes Craig recognized the pedestrian. It was the Clyde Tupper whose call had so troubled the Fogarty home; the Clyde Tupper who had so narrowly escaped bullets discharged from a speeding car outside the apartment house.

Had there been time, had he not been chained to the tiller, he would have leaped down and accosted Tupper. He would have demanded why the man was there, in that place, obviously so interested in the building where the fire had been, obviously in a rage. He would have asked Tupper what caused that rage. But, because that course of action was impossible, Craig stored the incident in his retentive mind, so that, in a year or in five years, he would be able to describe Tupper, recite his expressions of countenance, and the expressive, disgruntled movements of arms and body. For Mr. Tupper something had gone amiss. As the ladder started and his hands were firm on the tiller, he wondered if Tupper's unhappy state of mind were connected with the extinct fire. Craig frowned. Could his displeasure be because the fire had so promptly become extinct? A fire which the Marshal, shouting to Chief Fogarty, had said was a stinker. To Craig it had seemed a stinker. It was elementary that innocent fires do not start in half a dozen places at once. That one fact was sufficient to establish evidence of arson so strong as to be almost conclusive.

He chewed over this morsel mentally until he reached the engine house, and continued to masticate it as he stripped and got under the shower and applied soothing ointment to his burns. Then he went down to the kitchen where the aroma of coffee was most welcome to his nose, and filled a cup and sat down at the table.

"What did you boys think of it?" he asked, his voice hoarse, almost a croak.

"A torch done it," Dodd said, and expressed his opinion of arsonists.

"Seems like," said another fireman.

"Sloppy job of it," Dodd criticized.

"Firebug?" asked Craig.

Dodd, who had been on the force a dozen years, and whose opinion was worth listening to, shook his head. "Firebugs don't mostly work in lofts," he said. "It was a torch."

"Not a pro," said another fireman. "Too sloppy. I'd say an amateur—or maybe a learner."

"I read in the paper yesterday," Craig said, "that there is no organized, professional arson in New York."

"Not like in the Depression, maybe," Dodd answered, "but I bet you can hire a bozo with a candle and a bottle of gasoline."

"Or a dose of nitrocellulose. . . . Or maybe a dab of phosphorus."

24

Dodd, the statistician, said, "There were two hundred and four known incendiary fires in 1955. It ain't exactly arson, but there was 2,672 fires started by malicious boys. Them juvenile delinquents you hear talk about."

"More families ought to own razor straps," Craig said. "If there were more lads with sore behinds at home, there'd be less nasty mischief abroad."

Chief Fogarty came into the room, begrimed and out on his feet. A cup of coffee was set before him and he gulped it thirstily.

"Hadn't you better get doctored?" Craig asked solicitously.

"I'm able yit," the Chief said morosely, "to cope with a little swallow of smoke."

Craig followed the elder man out of the room. Fogarty turned on him angrily. "For why are you doggin' my footsteps?" he demanded.

"Just thought you ought to know," Craig said, "Clyde Tupper was prowling the street outside the fire."

"And what of it?" demanded Chief Fogarty. "What skin is that off your butt?"

"None, sir," Craig said stiffly. "Nor was it my business that Nora and I watched while he got shot at as he came out of your apartment the other night."

"You," the Chief said savagely, "and that snoopin' daughter of mine had best cease and desist from pokin' your snoots into what don't concern you."

"Anything, sir, that concerns you does concern Nora and me," Craig said sturdily. "And anything that stinks of arson concerns me, who am about to become a fire marshal."

The Chief's erect shoulders slumped; his straight back seemed to lose its stiffness, and without another word he turned and ascended the stairway as if it were a toilsome climb.

CHAPTER FOUR

CRAIG BATTS was assigned temporarily to theater duty. He knew he was required to report at the Century Theatre properly uniformed and with badge a half hour before the start of the performance. He recorded in the company journal the time of his departure, as he would record his return to the station within half an hour of the end of the show. Once in the building he followed rigorous routine. He knew the location of the nearest street alarm box. His first act on entering the theater was to transmit over the inside alarm box test signal 11. After that he inspected emergency exits, stairways and passages and fire doors and sprinkler systems. He must hunt for accumulated rubbish understage, close all doors in the proscenium walls, see to it there was no smoking backstage. At the end of the performance he must see to the lowering of the asbestos curtain, and at all times be ready, in case of fire, to appear before the audience to prevent panic. The regulations specifically informed him he was not there to watch the show.

The offering at the Century was a musical revue, elaborate, spectacular, with gorgeous costumes and scenery. It was a large company with show girls and little girls who did precision routines. So there was constant movement and congestion in the wings as act succeeded act and men and girls scurried to make quick costume changes. Craig, having finished his routine, occupied a chair out of the way against the wall and watched with keen interest the movement of this artificial world. He had performed similar duty before but always in a house offering drama to the public, so this experience was novel to that trick mind of his which, whether he wanted it to or not, stored away in its mysterious recesses myriads of details.

He had, of course, gone to the theater and seen comics and artistes and scantily clad chorus girls across the footlights. But to be shouldered about and surrounded by lovely young women whose bodies were concealed only so much as was required by law was another thing. To stand against a wall out of the way while he was surrounded by a group of practically nude chorus girls, unconscious of him and of their almost nudity, was at first embarrassing, but then became commonplace—normal in this abnormal universe. He reflected that probably an hour in some nudist camp would suffice to dissipate the consciousness of nakedness and the acceptance of bare flesh as something commonplace and run-of-mine.

It was the middle of the first act before anyone spoke to him, and then it was a young woman who stood on one foot while she leaned against the bricks and held the other foot in her hands to knead it. He noticed that while her hair was black as jet her eyes were violet. She was only a couple of inches over five feet tall. Her small face, so close to him, looked a bit grotesque with its necessary make-up. She sighed and grimaced and then caught his eyes upon her.

"Hello, fireman," she said, and then, "Oh, my aching feet!"

Craig said nothing, not thinking of anything to say.

"I inherit aching feet," she said wryly. "My dad was a cop. Pounding pavements. You firemen got the best of it—you ride. . . . You're a new one, aren't you?"

"I'm temporary," he told her.

She peered at him curiously. "I don't guess," she said, "I'd care to marry a fireman."

"No?" he said. "And why not? We're pretty desirable. Steady pay and pension. So pursued are we that we must make ourselves hard to get."

The girl raised her voice as she shifted to the other leg and massaged the opposite foot. "Hi, Gertie," she called to another girl a dozen feet away, "come get a piece of this. He's a card that gives off comical sayings."

"You keep him, Annie," said the other girl. "Firemen can't afford minks."

27

"The reason," Annie said to Craig, continuing to rub her foot, "that I wouldn't marry a fireman is they don't get home nights."

"How many nights does a chorine get home?" he retorted.

"But we're there all day except matinees." She put on her slipper and lowered her foot to the stage.

Craig never had, until now, exchanged a word with a chorus girl. He knew nothing about chorus girls, but in common with all too many people he had a hazy idea that they were amoral young women who displayed their physical equipment mainly for the purpose of attracting sugar daddies or acquiring apartments on Park Avenue. Now, as, at close range, he saw them going about their business methodically, painstakingly—probably with aching feet—he wondered if this was necessarily so. It was conceivable that being a chorus girl was a job like being a fireman or a policeman or a truck driver or a teller in a bank, and that they cavorted in attractive seminudity, not because of any personal desire to exhibit themselves, but because it was written that way in the script. And, quite possibly, that they could be as modest at home as other girls who earned a living as stenographers or salesgirls or baby sitters. He let his mind turn to beaches in the summer, and his logical intellect jumped him to the conclusion that even the nicest girls delight in cavorting slightly clad before the public eye. What, he asked himself, was the difference between making such an appearance for fun at the seashore or for a livelihood on the stage? Then his mind strayed to the imponderable, and he propounded a philosophical question to himself: What is modesty?

"Cat got your tongue?" Annie asked pertly.

"Do you have a family?" he asked.

"Sure. Ma and pa and three kid sisters."

His inquiring mind urged him to persist in questioning: to ask about her home life, her interests away from the stage, her ambitions, but he did not know how to go about it without being brash. She helped out.

"That's one of my kid sisters yonder," she said. "She's eighteen. Now I ask you, Mr. Fireman, isn't she a dish?"

The little girl Annie indicated, just coming down the iron stairway, was indeed a dish. Annie was a more than ordinarily pretty girl, as she would have to be; but little sister was something special. She had what the French call *beauté de diable*, a foreign phrase

28

with which Craig was unacquainted. But he could have expressed the same thing in less elegant language. This child was exquisite. Even under the make-up her little face was one not to be forgotten. She seemed to move with a special grace, and even among those dozens of girls selected for shapeliness, she stood out as a masterpiece of sculpture stands out among concrete garden statues. Craig expelled a breath.

"Gosh!" he exclaimed.

"That's what they all say," Annie said acidly. "She's a doll, and if you think I'm jealous, you're nuts. . . . She's my baby sister and I'm supposed to keep an eye on her. . . . How'd you like that for an assignment, Mr. Fireman?"

"She looks," said Craig in an odd voice, "like an Irish angel."

"And because she is," Annie said grimly, "there lies her danger. To her the wor-rld is a garden." For the first time there was an Irish roll to Annie's *r*. "All nice smell and pretty flowers. With no thought that a skunk may lurk in the foliage." The corner of her lip lifted. "She knows nothing, and if you try to tell her she shies away like a scairt kitten. . . . And every wolf from the Battery to the Bronx crouchin' in the bushes to pounce!"

Suddenly Annie darted away to take her place in a line of girls about to make their entrance, leaving Craig with thoughts. He was not sure he was not violating regulations when he talked to a member of the company, but upon this point there was nothing specific in the book. He gave himself the benefit of the doubt.

He sat now amusing himself by striving to photograph upon the plate of his mind the kaleidoscopic movement taking place before him, so that he could remember and recite its details in the future. It was difficult, baffling because there were so many elements, so many comings and goings. He closed his eyes and tried to recall what had taken place during the past five minutes. Then he opened his eyes again to observe, and did so just in time to see a man coming upon the stage from the direction of the stage door. Craig blinked, for the last thing in the world he had anticipated was to see this man here. It was Mr. Tupper, Homburg in hand, so that his bristling hair was visible. He was in a beautifully tailored dinner jacket, and no bulge was visible under his left armpit. He was sleek, handsome and seemed to be sure of himself in these surroundings, coming in as if he had a right to be there. And, arrogantly, almost as if he deliberately flouted the law, he was smoking a cigarette. Craig got up from his chair and confronted the man.

"No smoking backstage," he said officially.

Tupper lowered a brow and said unpleasantly, "Who says so?"

"The law says so," Craig said with that courtesy which he had been taught to show the public.

"And if I do?" Tupper asked. Craig could smell liquor on his breath.

"Then I shall notify the stage manager," Craig said, "and if you persist the theater inspector."

Tupper shrugged as if it were not worth making an issue. Then he narrowed his eyes and peered at Craig. He was not drunk, but he was well on in liquor, in a condition to be unpleasant, even belligerent.

"I've seen you before," he said.

"Possibly," Craig answered. He had done his duty and was about to turn away and resume his chair; but Tupper would not have it that way.

"I remember," he said. "At Old Man Fogarty's."

"At Chief Fogarty's," Craig corrected stiffly.

"He's what I choose to call him," Tupper said loudly, and there were hushes from stagehands to warn and quiet him. He held his open hand before Craig's nose and slowly closed his fingers. "In there I have him," he said. "Just like that."

"Mr. Tupper," Craig said, "I am the fireman on duty here. I can take notice of nothing of a personal nature. It will be well if you do not create a disturbance."

Tupper hesitated as if of half a mind to take unpleasant action. Then he shrugged again. "Could be I'll look you up," he said. "Could be."

He turned on his patent-leather heel and walked forward, standing where he could get a view of the action on the stage. Presently the chorus danced off, Annie's glowing little sister among the last to exit. Craig, from his tilted chair, heard Tupper utter a low exclamation and saw him thrust his head forward. The man's big hand thrust itself out and not gently grasped the little girl's bare shoulder.

"Hi, Jail Bait," he said, "come to Papa. You're a new one. What's your name, Sugar?"

She uttered a little, startled cry and tried to draw away, but he

30

clung to her, a half-drunken leer on his handsome face. His grin was vulpine as he bent toward her. "I'll be waiting after the show," he said. "Ask any of the girls. I rate high with the babes."

Craig's hands doubled into fists. His knuckles were white, but he did not move from his chair. He was not there to rescue damsels in distress. He was a member of the fire department on important duty. The audience beyond the footlights was his responsibility which he must not neglect for any reason. Much as this half-intoxicated bounder needed a lesson, Craig must not administer it. It was not thought of personal consequences to himself if he indulged in a public fracas with a civilian, but he had been trained and drilled to adhere to a rigid code. That code required that his obligations as a fireman take precedence over all things. But he did, privately, determine that he would seek a day and an opportunity when it would be permissible to discuss this and another thing with Clyde Tupper.

But Craig need not have intervened. Suddenly the air was full of kicking, clawing arms and legs as Annie launched herself upon this man who had annoyed little sister. She kicked, scratched, bit—but even in her fury she was silent as a trouper should be. It was a still fury; she was careful not to disturb the performance behind the lights. Her red nails raked his face; her tiny feet kicked his shins, and she hissed at him like some furious little king bird attacking an eagle.

"You!" she panted. "You big evil tomcat." He tried to extricate himself, but she followed tenaciously. "Just you make one more pass at my sister and you'll get it. . . ." She drew back, gasping for breath, unconscious of the members of the company who crowded around them, staring. She stood now, white and deadly calm. "I know you, Tupper," she said almost in a whisper. "With good reason. If harm comes to my sister by you, I'll kill you. Hear me, I'll kill you."

The concerned stage manager pushed his way to her side, scowling at Tupper, throwing a protective arm about Annie's shoulders. "What goes on here?" he demanded. "Behave yourself, Annie. There's a show going on. And you, Tupper, I've warned you before. Drag out of here. Go home and sleep it off."

"Don't heave your weight around, Manning," Tupper said, blustering but making no hostile movement.

"I don't like you, Tupper, nor your kind," Manning said. "If I had my way, you never would get past the stage door."

"But I get past," Tupper sneered.

Manning nodded. "Someday," he said softly, "you'll get past it once too often. . . . Now scram before you get tossed with a thick ear."

Craig relaxed. He had been teetering on the razor edge between the restraint placed upon him by his duty and his impulses as a human being. He could not have taken much more without forgetting his badge and uniform. His knuckles were white and his muscles tense as he fought for self-control, and it was with a sigh of relief that he saw Tupper escorted to the stage door by the stage manager.

For a moment he sat there oblivious to Annie and her little sister; to the members of the troupe and stagehands; to everything but himself and Clyde Tupper. It was as if they two were the sole inhabitants of the world. It was strange, a psychic thing. Almost prescience. For it came to him that he and Tupper were enemies à outrance. That, perhaps millenniums before either was born, it was predestined that they would someday live and hate. It was written that they should meet and that only one of them would survive their ultimate meeting. In a curious way it was crystal clear to him that, if one had been born at the South Pole and the other at the North Pole, their destinies would have drawn them together. Of this much he was certain; of so much protest he was capable. But further his glimpse into the future did not penetrate. He was not told which of the two would emerge from that final meeting with a whole skin.

The group dissipated. Craig heard one girl say to another, "Annie sure got her Irish up."

"I wouldn't be in that wolf's shoes if he goes tampering with the kid sister," said her companion. "Annie's a cookie that plays for keeps."

The performance terminated. The curtain descended. Craig, as required, saw to the lowering of the asbestos curtain, made certain that all trap doors were closed and all elevators made flush with the stage floor. He left the theater by the stage door and returned to the engine house, where he signed in on the log. He went back past the huge red ambulance to the kitchen, where he took a good-night cup of coffee before he climbed to the dormitory. There he removed his clothes and laid them out in the required manner before he climbed between the cool sheets. But sleep did not come at once. He could not rid his mind of Clyde Tupper, of Annie's little sister and of his almost father, Chief Fogarty. He did not think of Nora. Probably this was because they were so much like brother and sister that she was negligible. That power of prophecy which had rested upon him so briefly did not manifest itself again. It did not so much as hint that his fraternal feeling toward Nora Fogarty was by no means a permanent thing, and that it might be altered suddenly and radically.

CHAPTER FIVE

A GENTLEMAN of middle age with waving gray hair brushed back from a high, narrow forehead was seated at the table having a cup of coffee with Craig Batts and a couple of other members of the company. A monocle dangled from a black ribbon. He was exquisitely tailored, pink of cheeks as if from skillful massage, and pearl-gray spats covered his slim ankles. If one had been seeking a model for an aristocratic gentleman of the nineties, Pieter Van Rensselaer would have been incredibly exact for the part. Also, incredibly, this dapper member of the socially elect was a bluff. There never was a day when he would not desert a Lucullan luncheon at the Racket Club, or a box in the opera, to go rushing off to answer a fire alarm in any one of New York's boroughs. He was an *aficionado*. Some gentlemen might be fanatical first-nighters; others might water at the mouth at sight of a Van Gogh, or experience palpitations in the presence of a Chien Lung ceramic, but Pieter Van Rensselaer's heart went pit-a-pat at the sound of a siren.

From coast to coast there exist a multitude of buffs, whose only animal equivalent was the spotted coach dog who used to run to fires under the very hoofs of fire-engine horses—a species now unhappily extinguished by mechanization.

There is, in more antiquarian circles of the fire department, a great argument over the origin of the word "buff." It came into being a century or more ago in the day of the volunteer fire companies among which was high rivalry even to the point of mayhem. It was the custom of these companies, upon the alarm of fire, to send out a fleet, hard-bitten member carrying a keg. This he would put over the hydrant and stand alongside to defend it, so that his own company might be first to affix a hose and turn its stream on the fire. These companies grew tougher and tougher until they degenerated into the first gangs of New York. Now a buff is held by some authorities originally to have been a boy who hung around the engine house wearing a stylish buffalo-skin cap. Other sapient historians claim the word derives from the color of the uniforms of the militia of that day. The latter is the opinion of the learned librarian of the department's amazing collection of books, manuscripts and newspapers over in the college and museum in Long Island City.

But Pieter Van Rensselaer was a *rara avis* even among fire fanatics. He was a bosom friend of mayors and commissioners. He carried proudly in a leather case a gold badge conferring upon him honorary rank, and, of course, there never had been a gentleman of such wealth and social position and influence to claim membership in the fellowship of buffs.

He would rather breakfast with a buttman or nozzleman or Johnny-come-lately in a fire engine house than eat oatmeal and flapjacks with the President in the White House. Nevertheless, eccentric as your run-of-the mine citizen might deem him to be, he was popular with the members of the department, which marked him as quite a person, because you have to be all wool and a yard wide to gain the esteem of the city's fire fighters.

His meticulously kept scrapbook of clippings would one day be of high value to the library. It was an expense not to be afforded by one of moderate means. Clipping services supplied him with every reference to fires or firemen published in the United States. It was his declared purpose, when old age and stiffened legs overtook him, to write a comprehensive history of fire from the day it was first produced by rubbing two sticks together to the era of isotopes.

Now he was spreading on the bare boards of the table a number of clippings from newspapers.

"I call your attention, young gentlemen," he said with the air of a pedant, "to these bits of paper. Their datelines are from Dallas, Cincinnati, Denver, Omaha, New Orleans. Coincidence, of course, is possible in this haphazard world. One repetition of an event may be a coincidence. Two repetitions arouse suspicion in the logical mind. Three repetitions abut upon the marvelous. But the fourth repetition establishes either a scientific law or an efficient plan."

This was a bit esoteric for Craig, but he reserved his questions while Pieter continued earnestly. "Each of these fires," he said solemnly, "occurred in a building in close proximity to a bank or a jewelry store. In each instance, during the confusion incident to a fire, the bank or the store was looted. In each case there was suspicion of arson, but no evidence that could be taken to court."

"Yes, sir," Craig said deferentially. "And what do you deduce from this?"

"It indicates to me," said Pieter, "organization."

"Do you mean an arson organization? But, sir, we were told the other day that there is no commercial arson."

"Fiddledeedee," said Pieter scornfully. "Arson we have always with us. And so long as there is business failure, hatred, jealousy, there will always be arson. If there is a market for arson, then there will be bad men who will supply the demand. There will be arsonists for hire."

"But this, sir, would indicate hired arson on a large scale—a business that ramifies from Coast to Gulf to Midwest."

"To me," said Pieter, "that is the deduction. But it goes further than mere arson for hire. These clippings prove to me that there is also arson as an aid to looting. A combination might exist whose purpose is to set fires as a distraction, to cause confusion making it possible to commit, under cover of excitement and noise and fire and smoke, opportunities to break and enter and rob."

"Have you, sir, called this to the attention of the Commissioner?"

"Indeed I have. He is, to put it mildly, skeptical."

"How about the Chief Fire Marshal?"

"I think, Batts"—Pieter knew almost every fireman by name—"that he was impressed but reluctant to admit it."

"Do you see, sir, a sort of company with local branches?"

"I doubt that. Affiliations possibly. No. What I envision is a sort of traveling circus of experts. Expert arsonists, expert safecrackers, expert thieves and robbers. Such a troupe, with no local connections, who dropped into town for a depredation and then vanished would be pretty difficult to identify unless caught in the act. Constantly on the move. Flitting. A hit-and-run process."

He finished his coffee, dropped his monocle from his eye and picked up his malacca walking stick. In the door he paused and turned and motioned to Craig. "A word with you, Batts," he said.

Craig accompanied him past the apparatus to the sidewalk. "Batts," the dapper man said earnestly, "Chief Fogarty worries me."

"In what way, sir?"

"Suddenly he seems to have aged. As if there were a hidden illness or a grave mental disturbance. Are you aware of it?"

"He is not as young as he used to be," Craig answered noncommittally.

"He has been almost a father to you."

"No father could have done more for me."

"Then keep a loving eye on him, young man. His manner, his expression when he thinks himself unobserved, I do not like. . . . If—should you feel that there is need for something—for some assistance—do not hesitate to call upon me. Chief Fogarty and I are longtime friends."

"Thank you, sir. I will not forget your offer."

Van Rensselaer walked jauntily down the street, wholly unconscious that he was an anachronism, a sort of living ghost from the days of the Four Hundred and Mrs. Astor and Booth and Barrett and Barnum's Museum. Unique as he was, he attracted little attention. New York is so crammed with oddities that one more causes no furore.

Chief Fogarty came clumping down the narrow stairs from his office and waggled a peremptory finger at Craig Batts. "Young spriggins," he said tartly, "you are to rayport forthwith to the Chief Fire Marshal at the man's office on the eleventh floor of the Municipal Building on Chambers Street."

This direction was so redundant that Craig perceived that Chief Fogarty was in an emotional state and sought to conceal it with many useless words.

"Does this mean, sir, that I—?"

"It means, most like," said the Chief, "that you will be layin' aside your uniform and your cap and your badge, maybe foriver. That ye will cease to be a fireman like your father and mesilf. It is a serious thing. It is a break wit' family tradition. . . . Fogartys

37

and Battses was born to fight fires, not to snoop in the ashes to find how they were touched off." He knuckled his eyes. "The young will be young; and new ways push aside ways that are old. Maybe 'tis well to be so."

"I hope it will be well," Craig said gravely.

"Good luck be with you, lad, and bad cess to all that impede you. This must not pull ye away from Nora and me, for changes often cause sad separations. And new friends at hand cause old friends at a distance to be forgot."

"Never fear that, Uncle Paddy," Craig said harshly. "That day you'll never see. . . . How about I come to supper tonight and tell you how it went?"

Uncle Paddy nodded his head jerkily. "Good luck to ye, boy. I shall miss ye sore."

So Craig, not sure yet that he must say good-by to his companions in the firehouse, took the subway down to the great building on Chambers Street, with its wide high arch through the middle where it straddled the street. The elevator carried him swiftly to the eleventh floor, and he walked through the entrance to the offices of the department. He gave his name to the uniformed man at the reception desk and presently was admitted to the office of the Chief Marshal. The Marshal's aide at his desk in the outer office motioned for him to enter the inner room. Signals were pinging from the loud-speaker while the Chief cocked his head birdlike to listen. When silence came he turned his grizzled head to peer up with icy gray eyes at the young fireman.

"Batts," he said inclemently. "You're Batts that does memory tricks."

Craig saw no reason to make answer to this.

"Quicker than I figured, a vacancy has come. I shall offer it to you. Before you say yes or no I'll have a word with you."

"Yes, sir," said Craig.

"You come to us from the uniformed ranks," the Chief said. "It is not an advantage to you. Do ye know, young man, that a marshal brought here from the uniformed ranks can never rise to be Chief Marshal or even supervisor? Such is the law, though I do not understand why. A civilian alone can win promotion in the Bureau of Fire Investigation."

"I am aware of that, sir."

"But it does not prevent you from taking the examination for promotion to lieutenant or beyond in the regular department. We have here a marshal who is a lieutenant. But should ye turn out to be the greatest fire detective that ever lived, ye cannot hope ever to sit in my chair."

"I understand, sir."

"And ye still wish for the transfer?"

"I do."

"In that case you will report here in the morning, having laid aside your uniform, and your training will commence. My aide in the outer room is also a supervisor. He will start you on your way."

"Thank you, sir," Craig said earnestly.

"Here there is no checker playing or time for coffee. You will sleep at home. From now on you will never be sure of a free moment for fun or frolic. You will be liable to sudden call at all times. When ye go out of this office on duty you will call in and report your whereabouts every hour and a half. Little private life will be yours. It is a strict duty. Report to my aide at eight o'clock."

"Thank you, sir," Craig said and walked out of the office.

The young man at the flat-topped desk outside looked up at him and smiled in a friendly way.

"See you in the morning, Batts. In civilian clothes."

Craig returned to his engine house, collected his personal belongings, said good-by to his comrades and went home. He was conscious as he rode the subway to Brooklyn that he had reached the first important fork in the road of his life and had selected with open eyes which direction he would take. To have taken the other path, the one his father had followed and Uncle Paddy, would undoubtedly have brought him promotions, increases in salary and in the end an ample pension. The way he had chosen had less to offer in a material way, but he was content. There was something almost mystic in his elation—almost as if he were conscious that this change had been predestined. But the point that gave him highest satisfaction was that he felt he had found a niche into which he fitted perfectly.

Craig had a figure which satisfactorily filled a finely tailored gabardine suit. It was an extravagance. Though his opportunities to disport himself in civilian clothes had been few, nevertheless a certain vanity had urged him to select the best his purse could afford. Now that he had laid aside his blue uniform forever, he put on his new habiliments with juvenile satisfaction. He studied as much of himself as he could make visible in his mirror and was justified in a sensation which was the opposite of disappointment.

The shirt and tie and shoes and socks which completed his outfit were not worn to trap the admiration of the beholder but for his own satisfaction. He gave slight thought to the fact that he was about to dine with a young lady, because the young lady was nobody but Nora Fogarty. Now, if it had been some other girl!

His was a walk-up apartment. He descended the stairs and, well before the supper hour, turned his steps toward the Fogartys' flat. Nora, her gown protected by an apron, opened the door and stood peering up at him as if she did not recognize him. Even if it was only Nora he preened himself. She cocked her head pertly and wrinkled her nose.

"It's the same face," she said, "but a different set of feathers. Have you quit the department to become a tailor's dummy?"

"Hush your noise before I give you the back of my hand," he retorted. "I'm done with the uniform forever."

"It was man's clothing," she said.

"It's not the color of the cloth that counts, but what's underneath it."

"Do you say so now," she said, pretending to a brogue which was not natural to her, in order to deride him. "And what's underneath this wolf's clothing?"

"A fire marshal this day appointed," he said, as she stepped aside to let him enter.

"So you got it!" she said, and there was a look in her violet eyes which he did not perceive and which, had he seen it, he would not have understood. "What good luck for the Bureau of Fire Investigation. I hope 'twill be worthy of your talents."

He tossed his soft hat on a table and turned to her, staring down at her with puzzled eyes.

"Why do you always belittle me?" he asked. It was the first time he had heeded it. Always before it had been a natural part of the bickering of children who had grown up together.

"Because," she said sharply, and tears were close to her lids, "you are a great, blind, stupid dolt that makes me so irritated I could spit."

40

"That," he said with a grin, "is inelegant."

"Someday, my lad," she told him, "you will rile me to the point where I'll show you what inelegance is."

"Listen, Sugar Bun," he said seriously, "you speak as if you mean it. Are you mad with me? What, now, have I done that's wrong?"

She turned her back and flirted her skirts so that for a split second a lovely leg was visible. "Get you a can of beer out of the icebox," she directed. "I've the supper to get ready." She paused in the dining-room door and peered back at him over her shoulder. "I could count on one hand the times I've seen you out of uniform," she said. "It's a stranger you seem to me."

The telephone rang and Nora crossed the room to lift it from its cradle. "Hello," she said.

"Is this Miss Fogarty?"

"Nora Fogarty," she replied.

"This is Jack Mellon speakin'. Your father's aide. I've ill news for you. The Chief was hurt. They took him to the hospital."

"Is—is he bad?"

"The particulars I do not know," said Mellon evasively. "He was took to Bellevue. Shall I come for you with his car?"

"It will save time if I take a cab," she said steadily and hung up the instrument. She turned a white, stricken face to Craig Batts.

"Father's hurt and taken to Bellevue," she said in a brittle voice.

She ran into the kitchen and turned off the stove. She tore off her apron, and, without waiting for hat or bag or gloves, made for the door. Craig was beside her. In the street they were fortunate that a vacant cab was passing.

"Bellevue Hospital," said Craig tensely, "and fast. I pay the fines if any."

CHAPTER SIX

AT THE great hospital they were told that Chief Fogarty could not be seen; that his condition was critical. Other than that the authorities reserved what information they possessed. The manner of the intern who spoke with Nora was peculiar. He was an important young man whose manner seemed to assert that he was big with some secret which he was forbidden to divulge.

"Is Father conscious?" Nora asked.

"His condition," evaded the young doctor, "is as satisfactory as could be hoped at this early stage."

"Was it," Craig asked with some impatience, "smoke poisoning?"

"With complications," said the important young man. "I advise you to go home and await developments."

"And I," Craig said grimly, "advise you to find a new manner toward anxious people who inquire. You might earn yourself a belt in the nose."

Before the intern could retort two men entered the reception room. The shorter, grizzled one strode up to the desk and announced that he was Deputy Chief Fire Marshal in a voice of authority. "And this is the medical officer in charge. We will be taken at once to Chief Fogarty."

The receptionist turned to the young intern for directions. That young man, less bumptious now in the presence of impressive authority, said nervously, "But, Chief, he is in the operating room."

The medical officer turned to the Deputy Chief. "There'll be nothing for you yet," he said. Then to the intern, "You will take me to the operating room."

42

"Oh, Doctor!" exclaimed Nora.

"Yes," he said, frowning.

"I'm his daughter, sir."

His face softened. "Be as easy as you can, my dear," he said. "I'm here to see that nothing is left undone. The department looks after its own. Wait if you like. I will send down word to you as soon as there is word to send."

The Deputy Chief, face set and stern, turned to the young people. "You are Paddy Fogarty's daughter?" he demanded.

"Yes, sir."

"And this young man?"

"I'm Craig Batts, sir. Uncle Paddy has been a father to me."

"Batts. . . . Batts. . . . And are ye the new appointed fire marshal?"

"To report in the morning," Craig said.

"Where," the Deputy Chief demanded of the receptionist, "can we sit and be private?"

They were shown into a small room with chairs and a sofa. Craig ventured to speak to his superior. "You would not be here, sir, if this were an ordinary injury."

"I would not," the Deputy Chief replied. "It was a blaze set by a torch." His lips were compressed and his manner boded ill for some criminal. "Which is not the worst of it, child. Your father was struck down by one seeking to take his life."

"You would know, sir," Batts said, "that my own father died in the same way."

"I would," the Deputy Chief said shortly, "but Paddy Fogarty is not yet dead. Not by a long ways. Nor will he be, I hope, with his name in the Commissioner's report with a black line around it. . . ." His heavy hand touched Nora's arm lightly. "It is best you go home, child, in the knowledge that all will be done that can be done. And the first good word that comes will be sent to you. . . . The prayers of a good girl like you may work a miracle."

Craig rode home with Nora in a cab. She was not crying, but calm and still. He went upstairs with her and unlocked and opened the door.

"You must eat," he said.

"We both must eat," she replied, and walked steadily into the kitchen where she rescued as much of the supper as was possible.

43

"It's the waiting," she said through stiff lips.

"Cupcake," he said, his firm fingers gripping her shoulder, "I've a feeling. The four fives will not be struck for him this time."

She threw her arms around him and sobbed with great, convulsive sobs on his breast. Then she drew away, shook her head vigorously. "Do not go," she said. "I fear to be alone."

He slept that night in a long nightgown belonging to Uncle Paddy—on the davenport in the living room. It was daylight when the telephone awakened him and he reached it before Nora could come out of her room. The voice was the voice of Jack Mellon, Chief Fogarty's aide.

"Who is this?" Mellon asked.

"Craig Batts."

"Tell his girl," Mellon said, "that there is good hope. He is not conscious yet but, barring what cannot be foreseen, he will pull through. It's a concussion and the smoke. But the doctors have hope."

"Is he like to regain consciousness?"

"When they do not predict."

"Thank you, Mellon," Craig said, and gave the word to Nora.

"After breakfast," she said, "when you report downtown, I will go to the hospital and wait there."

So after coffee and toast and eggs Craig escorted her to the hospital and then went on himself to the Municipal Building and reported to the office of the Chief Marshal. The Chief's aide, who, incidentally, had just received his Master's degree after long night study at New York University, took Batts down the corridor and opened a door into a room occupied by a couple of secretaries, and then into a second large room where a number of men sat at desks busy with reports. These men, mostly youngish, were marshals on duty in Manhattan and the Bronx. Craig could see a similar room beyond where sat the marshals assigned to the other boroughs of the city. Around the walls stood steel filing cabinets containing the files of investigations made by the Bureau of Fire Investigation. He was introduced to the men with whom he would work, and left with Supervisor Wilkins.

"First," said his mentor, "you will spend time with our files. You will study them to learn methods and procedures. You will learn what you are like to find and how it is to be dealt with. After you are so grounded, you will go out with an experienced marshal to learn by doing. You will learn how to make out the three cards— the Report of Deaths at Fires; the Report of Injuries at Fires, and the general card of report on investigated fires. There will also be lectures and instructions from time to time until you have learned to be an assistant fire marshal. You will then have your foundation."

He was assigned to a desk and records of investigations were placed before him. Covertly he looked about him at the men with whom he was to work. Each man occupied a small, flat-topped desk, and most of them were busy with pen and paper. It might have been an office in some factory and the marshals might have been clerks. There was no hurry, no signs of excitement. The faces Craig studied were clean-cut and alert. That tenacious memory of his remembered their names. He opened the first folder and read the preliminary report card giving the bare facts of location, class of structure, number of stories, amount of damage and insurance, if there had been previous fires. On the reverse side was noted if there were suspicious circumstances and what testimony was taken. Then on other papers was set down the progress and manner of the investigation of the financial condition of the owner, his character, his books of record. Nothing glamorous, nothing exciting, all routine, but a meticulous, searching, efficient routine which resulted in the owner being brought to trial for arson and convicted to a long term in the penitentiary.

He learned, as he read, that the city was threatened by all too many pyromaniacs, most of them known to the Bureau. He learned how all too tender the courts were with these mentally deranged, and how, again and again, after being committed to some mental institution, they were released after a few weeks or months. He learned of the difficulty of producing evidence, not to indicate guilt but to prove guilt beyond a reasonable doubt. He learned how clever and perhaps unethical lawyers maneuvered to gain acquittals, and how it seemed almost as if the bar and the courts combined to frustrate the toils of the fire marshals.

After a day or two of this Craig turned to the man at the adjoining desk and said, "Seems as if you have to catch a man with a pail of gasoline in his hand and a lighted match before you can convict him."

"And then," said the assistant marshal, "some slick lawyer will prove it was cleaning fluid and ignited by a bolt of lightning."

The evenings he spent with Nora Fogarty. They visited the hospital nightly but were not yet permitted to see the Chief. He seemed to be holding his own well with brief periods of consciousness. The medical officer in charge, who personally was attending Chief Fogarty, was sanguine. "We'll have him out of here in a couple of weeks," he assured Nora.

It was not easy to induce Nora to leave their apartment lest some word should come from the hospital in her absence, but as her father's condition improved and her tension abated Craig did induce her to go to the neighborhood movie and stop in a nearby restaurant for a snack before going home. They were sitting at a table against the wall when a gentleman stopped in the aisle, removed his hat to display bristly hair *en brosse* and said solicitously, "Miss Fogarty, I was grieved to hear of your father's accident. I trust he is making good progress."

"It was no accident, Mr. Tupper," Nora said inclemently. "It was attempted murder."

His handsome face was deeply concerned. "That," he said, "is dreadful—unbelievable." He looked down at Craig Batts without recognition. "If there is something I can do—"

"There is nothing," she said shortly. "Except to leave my father alone when he comes home again."

"But I do not understand!" he exclaimed with raised brows. "My association with your father is greatly to his advantage."

"That," she said tersely, "is untrue."

"Miss Fogarty," he said blandly, "you are laboring under some queer misapprehension, of which I could disabuse your mind with a few minutes of explanation. If you would dine with me—"

It was here that Craig intervened. "I thought your specialty," he said, "was little chorus girls."

Tupper's bland expression vanished and his face became cold and menacing. "And who the hell," he demanded, "are you?"

"I," said Craig, "am the fireman who enjoyed seeing you get your face scratched in the theater the other night. I was sorry to be on duty."

"If you had not been on duty?" Tupper asked softly.

46

"You," said Craig, "would have been carried out instead of merely being invited to leave by the stage manager."

"Leave be, Craig," said Nora peremptorily.

"After one more word," Craig said evenly. "Miss Fogarty doesn't like you. I don't like you. Make no advances to her." Then he spoke unwisely, though he did not then know how unwise he was. His words derived from an aroused temper, perhaps from some unaccountable aroused instinct. "Leave little chorus girls alone, Tupper, and firemen's daughters. Stick to prowling around incendiary fires."

Tupper leaned over the table and his eyes were opaque, ophidian.

"Just what," he asked almost in a whisper, "did you mean by that?"

"Whatever you like," Craig answered.

He was surprised. He was prepared for violence. But there was no violence. The man Tupper turned on his heel, and without a further word strode to the front of the café and out into the street.

"Was that a good idea, Craig?" Nora asked.

"I liked it. I liked it fine," Craig said savagely.

"Remember," she said warningly, "he carries a gun."

"That," he said, "I'll bear in mind. . . . Shall we go home?"

He walked Nora back to the apartment and then went home to his own flat. In the morning he reported to headquarters and resumed the study of case histories. He returned to his desk early after a meager lunch. One of the supervisors was already at his desk. "Back early," he said to Craig.

"There's a special file I'd like to study. If it's permissible."

"What file is that, Batts?"

"The one on the fire where my father was killed," Craig said.

"And why would you want to see that?" asked the supervisor.

"There's little I was told at the time," Craig said. "I would like to know the facts."

"What was the date? Under what name would it be filed?"

Craig gave the required information, and the supervisor went to the filing cabinets. He opened a drawer and searched. His mouth puckered as he made more careful search.

"What's wrong?" Craig asked.

"That file," said the supervisor, "is missing."

"Misplaced?"

"In this Bureau," the supervisor said, "we don't misplace files."

"You mean?" Craig asked.

"I mean," the supervisor said gravely, "it has been abstracted."

"But why?" Craig asked. "Why would anybody steal that file about my father's death?"

"That," said the supervisor, "is a question we'll be ordered to find the answer for. The Chief Marshal must be told about this at once."

CHAPTER SEVEN

CURIOUS DIDOS were being cut on a forgotten block in the east Fifties. It was close to the river, and in these days was little used by traffic of any sort. Along its north side ran a high fence shutting off the rubble of a row of condemned and razed buildings, demolished to save taxes upon their uselessness. On the south side was a massive brick structure patterned somewhat after a castle on the Rhine. It had been a brewery, busy and prosperous back in the nineties, but standing these long years tenantless, with blind eyes staring lidless at the drab scene before it. Piercing its face at the right side were massive doors through which splendid Percherons had been wont to haul great wagons laden with kegs of beer. This barrier was again pierced by a smaller door, a sort of postern through which men might enter without the labor of swinging the massive portals.

It was inside this building pitiful in its desuetude that the curious didos were being cut. Four men in paint-splashed overalls were doing the cutting. They were putting the finishing touches upon the task of repainting an automobile. The color being applied was a brilliant red, and there were visible to the superficial eye such identifying marks as would permit it to masquerade successfully as the equipage of a Chief of the New York Fire Department.

Ready at hand were cans of paint of a sober black which would be used when the time came to repaint the car, covering the telltale red and returning it to civilian status. Though the four men wore working clothes they were provided with other garments—the uniforms of firemen, three helmets for men of the ranks and one white helmet for the pseudo-Chief. There were also rubber coats and boots. At hand and ready to be placed in the disguised car were four cases, each containing one of those weapons known to gangsterdom as tommy guns.

This place had been carefully selected as one where inquisitive eyes would not ask questions; and because it was not unhandy to a certain spot which was to be the objective of the meticulously planned depredation. There were few passers-by to note the comings and goings of the four men who, indeed, emerged but seldom but lived and ate their food and did their sleeping where they worked.

The didos even included a two-way radio system such as all official cars carry as equipment.

It was extremely unlikely that anyone would see this car emerge from the wide doors of the old brewery, or note its return to its hiding place. Within a matter of hours it would, after its return, cease to be red and become unnoticeable under a coat of somber black.

These several facts were, of course, unknown to the office of the Chief Fire Marshal of the City of New York, and were undreamed of by the force of men under his command. No man's imagination stretched so far as to envision such a viper's nest, and this was especially true of Craig Batts engrossed in his preliminary training.

He was fascinated by this tutelage and found it not irksome even when he found it involved a working knowledge of bookkeeping and accountancy. He found the case histories in the files, though terse and couched in stilted official language, to be engrossing, especially when he read between the lines to perceive the dogged persistence, the skilled investigation, the keen reasoning of the investigating fire marshals.

On the afternoon of his discovery that the file concerning the fire in which his father had lost his life was missing he was called into the small office of the Chief in Charge.

"Batts," asked that gentleman, "how did you come to discover that this particular file was missing?"

"I have been studying cases as directed," Craig answered. "Today I came back early from lunch because I wanted to read about that fire and the official findings on what happened to my father. I never knew the exact particulars."

"No," said the Chief abruptly. "The facts were not broadcast. How much have you talked about this matter?"

"Not at all, sir, after I reported it to the supervisor."

The Chief fixed him with inclement eye. "See that you keep a still tongue in your head," he ordered, dismissing Craig.

A duller mind than Craig's would have seen that this matter was regarded as important by his superiors, and that its implications were not agreeable. That a file, especially a file containing the findings in the investigation of the death of a Deputy Chief in Charge, was a matter demanding cautious and discreet handling. If the folder had merely been misplaced, it would be found. If it proved to have been abstracted, then there entered a sinister element intolerable to the integrity of the Bureau. There must exist a powerful reason for its theft. To Craig it was patent that there must be something in that file that constituted a peril to someone. It was even possible, he reasoned, that this peril had lain dormant until he, Craig Batts, had been placed in a position where he would have access to the files.

The perpetrator might well have guessed that Craig's curiosity would send him to read the contents of that folder and that this had made its abstraction necessary. If this were the truth, then a further and disturbing conclusion followed, namely that the guilty man had access, indeed, that he was a member of the corps of fire marshals inhabiting that office.

If these speculations presented themselves to Craig Batts's inexperience, how certain it would be that they were immediately apparent to his superiors who were by no means novices at reading evidence and making deductions from what they had read.

It was, presently, a welcome change from confinement within four walls to be assigned at last to that step in his training which would consist of minor investigations under the tutelage of an experienced marshal. The man who was to be his instructor was a saturnine individual with a cowlick, perhaps thirty-five years of age, whose acid and sometimes impious humor amused his comrades. His impiety was not directed against things religious but things human, and he had even been known to venture the shooting of verbal darts toward the Commissioner's office. His face, with ruddy cheeks, had an impish, impertinent cast, and when he looked at you it seemed always as if he were inwardly amused by something he saw not visible to other eyes. For all that, he was not an ill-natured young man, but gay and popular even in his most ironic moods.

"We're going out," he said, "to put salt on the tail of a pyro. This lad works when the moon is full. And he's got a quirk. His special talent is baby cabs in apartment hallways. Chucks in greasy rags, or excelsior, or something soaked in gasoline and touches it off. A month ago he did his little chore nine times in an area a half a mile square. He's extinct from moon to moon."

Craig tapped his forehead.

"Probably as sane as you or I," Priddy said, "till his night comes on him. Maybe he's got a grudge against baby cabs. Maybe he's a frustrated baby sitter." He contemplated that possibility. "Batts, I'm not maudlin about our civilization, and the two things that epitomize its decadence are baby sitters and dog walkers."

"You might," said Craig, "add prefabricated meals in tin cans."

"Comrade," Priddy said delightedly, "we see eye to eye. A world gone soft with gadgets and labor-saving doodads. And for what gain, I ask you, does the housewife avoid the cookstove and the washtub? What does she earn by burning the cookbook and wielding the can opener? What?"

"I'll bite," said Craig, "What?"

"A husband with ulcers, a baby that grows up to be a delinquent and an ambition to get rich quick on a quiz program. And while we're on that subject, what about a system that emits so many ghastly mental freaks? Who know offhand who manufactured the needle the camel walked through in the Bible?"

The morning's paper work had been completed when Priddy and Batts started upon their scouting expedition. At that time of day the pyromaniac would not be about his moonstruck business, but it would be efficient to scout the neighborhood, study at first hand the previous hallway fires; take a sort of census of baby carriages in hallways and do what was possible to reason out where the man would be most likely to strike his matches tonight. If they could discover a pattern, it would be helpful. They came up from the subway and took to the sidewalk which carried them past Number One Engine House on Thirty-first Street. Halfway down the block they heard warnings and saw the apparatus swing through the wide doors and swerve westward. This alarm of fire

52

might change the plans of the two assistant fire marshals, so Priddy went into the engine house and called the Fire Marshal's office to report their whereabouts.

"It's a three-bagger," said the answering voice over the telephone, using department argot for a three-alarm fire, and then, after a brief pause, it gave the location of the blaze and directions to proceed to the scene at once.

When they arrived the street was a jumble of ladders and towers and pumpers. An ambulance was there and the rescue wagon. Extension ladders already reared themselves against the face of the five-story building; smoke billowed from the windows of the third and fifth floors. It seemed a scene of inextricable confusion with firemen rushing about helter-skelter, but it was not confusion. Every piece of apparatus was where it should be; men in helmets and rubber coats and hats appeared to be running about like distracted ants from a disturbed anthill, but each one knew his task, kept out of the way of his fellows and went about his appointed work adeptly. The chaos was not chaos but system. The Senior Officer was somewhere inside assaying the fire and sending down to the street orders over the walkie-talkie carried by his aide. The first task was to insure ventilation; the second to get water on the flames.

The building was occupied by a dozen businesses of one sort or another—mostly small manufacturing concerns—crowded, huddled lofts. The fire had originated in the premises of a firm which processed feathers, but a second fire had unaccountably broken out two floors above in the workrooms of a company manufacturing cheap dresses. Two simultaneous fires on separated floors!

It was a neighborhood of antique shops, lofts, bookstores, but, as it neared Fifth Avenue, of more pretentious structures and concerns. There was an excellent furniture store, the sumptuous display room of a publisher, a first-rate tailor. Diagonally across from the burning building was the sedate front of the place of business of a nationally known jeweler.

Craig's trick brain was photographing the scene with all its intricate movement. He saw a red chief's car pick its way through apparatus and come to a stop at the curb. From it alighted four firemen, one wearing the white helmet of a chief. Instead of cross-

53

ing the street to the fire, they walked in a compact group across the sidewalk and into the jewelry store.

The interior of the shop was not visible from the street because of the backing of the display windows, and so the little squad passed from Craig's sight. Just why these firemen should hurry into the store Craig could not guess, but probably it was on some mission of protection or of prevention on special order to conserve what must have been a highly valuable stock-in-trade. But in his mind remained a picture of the episode even as he turned back to watch a flat hose being hoisted up the fire escape by means of the stretch.

Flames showed red and smoke issued from the fifth-story windows. A fireman emerged backward; he got his feet on the ladder secured by a safety device, and stood there in the smoke until a comrade passed to him a limp body which he slung across his shoulders and descended to the street. A waiting stretcher carried the casualty to the ambulance a hundred feet away.

Craig was aware of a dapper figure standing at his elbow, a slight man wearing a monocle in his eye, white spats on his ankles, and with a drooping, aristocratic, snowy mustache. He leaned upon a malacca walking stick and was as spick and span as if he had only that moment stepped from a bandbox. He peered at Craig a moment as if wondering how a person in civilian clothes could be permitted to loiter there, and then his patrician face lighted with recognition.

"Ah," he said, "the name is Batts, of course. Newly appointed fire marshal."

"Good day, Mr. Van Rensselaer," Craig responded courteously.

"I was," said the quaint old aristocrat, "enjoying my constitutional down Fifth Avenue when I heard the sirens. Naturally I dropped all other concerns and hastened to the scene of the fire. . . . It is not without points of interest."

With some vanity he took from his pocket a leather case which he opened to display a gold shield naming him to be an honorary chief of the fire department. "This," he explained, "permits me to pass all fire lines."

"What," asked Craig, "do you find of special interest here?"

"Fires," said the honorary chief, "do not commonly break out on two separated floors simultaneously."

54

"Could be a torch," Priddy said.

"Ah, indeed," said the old gentleman with a sly and sapient expression. "But then one seeks an explanation. Third floor and fifth floor! Would there be two separate, distinct and unrelated blazes? Possible. Possible but not probable. Two unrelated fires with two unrelated motives. Incredible. Or a double-barreled motive. I fancy, my young friend, that when you enter to investigate you will find evidence of arson. And I will hazard a guess that on each floor you will find similar evidence of arson."

"Quite possible," Priddy said.

"So fascinating," Van Rensselaer burbled, "if on both floors you were to discover that identical incendiary devices had been used."

"It sure would," Priddy agreed.

"And what, young gentlemen, would that phenomenon indicate?"

"Why, the same firebug," Priddy said.

"Rather more than that, I should reason," the old gentleman said shrewdly. "First, indication of plan, of pattern. . . . Would it be too farfetched to deduce that the twin fires are indeed a red herring?"

"That," Priddy said, "would be a whopping guess. A red herring is to set one off on a false trail."

"So it is. So it is. To distract attention. But to distract attention from what?"

Craig stood an instant as if frozen. He turned his head quickly to peer at the red chief's car parked at the curb in front of the jewelry store. And as he peered he noticed with that trick photographic brain of his that there was something irregular, a discrepancy. Something to be expected was not present. He astonished both Priddy and Van Rensselaer by shoving them brusquely aside. "Shake a foot," he snapped, and ran to the door of the store whose stock in trade was treasure. He was six feet from the entrance when the four firemen emerged, striding with military precision. Two of them carried canvas sacks that bulged.

"Stop there! . . . Stop!" Craig shouted, charging the quartet recklessly.

With more courage than discretion he lunged toward the four men. His reception was efficient. The two men walking side by side in front side-stepped with precision. Each grasped Craig by an arm and held him. One of the men in the rear raised his right hand, gripping a weapon known to the underworld as a sap, and brought it down once upon Craig's head. Then, not in panic but with precision, they crossed the walk to the door of their car, stepped inside, and before they could seat themselves the car moved forward swiftly, and then lurched down the street with siren screaming.

Priddy, taken wholly by surprise, bent over Craig and lifted his head which dropped limply over his arm.

Above the uproar a shrill voice could be heard imperiously summoning a stretcher. It was Pieter Van Rensselaer. He stood over Craig and Priddy, his aristocratic face sardonic. He spoke, but his words were addressed to no one in particular.

"I said red herring," he said pridefully. "And red herring it was."

Craig was carried to the ambulance. The red car had already shrieked its way to Fifth Avenue and turned north, as yet unpursued. Consciousness returned before Craig was laid on a bed, for his head was hard and his skull was thick. He struggled to sit up but sank back dizzily. "They looked alike," he said. "As alike as peas in a pod."

"Lie still," said the surgeon, pushing him back upon the pillow.

"Police!" Craig tried to shout.

"Just don't bother your pretty little head," said the surgeon.

Craig could not know it, but the police had been notified promptly by Priddy. Luke, immediately Craig had been carried away, went into the store where the clerks huddled, white-faced and bewildered.

"Assistant Fire Marshal Priddy," he said, displaying his identification. "What happened?"

"Four firemen came in," said an employee. "They separated and each one had a tommy gun. They ordered us to put up our hands. They pushed us back in a corner and looted the place."

"The vault?"

"That, too," said the man.

"They were firemen," squeaked a dapper clerk. "Firemen!"

"Don't be a fool," Priddy snapped. He peered about at smashed and denuded showcases. "Firemen, my aunt's calico cat. If you saw them again, could you identify them?"

They looked at each other queerly and then nodded in puzzled agreement. "They all looked exactly alike!"

"How alike?"

"Sort of," said a shivering clerk, "as if they weren't human. As if they were dead. Or wax."

"How much did they get away with?"

"How can we tell yet? Hundreds of thousands."

Police officers surged in and took charge. Priddy remained to give such information as he could after seeking the telephone and reporting to his superiors.

"Stay put till I get there," was the order he received.

He returned to the looted store, and as he did so there came in from the street mincingly the dapper figure of Pieter Van Rensselaer, jauntily swinging his malacca cane. He peered about him bird-like, and permitted his monocle to drop from his eye and dangle at the end of its ribbon.

"Neat," he said admiringly. "Neat, businesslike and artistic. You have been vouchsafed the privilege, Priddy, of being present at the production of a masterpiece. Er—trifles make perfection but perfection is no trifle. Some astute criminal brain merits congratulations." His turn was almost a pirouette as, with flourish of his cane, he made his exit to the disordered street.

CHAPTER EIGHT

IT WAS a stubborn, difficult fire. Choking gases, poisonous smoke were menaces. Before the fire flames were quenched three firemen were carried out gasping from fume poisoning. It was late evening before the fire marshals could move in to make their search for evidence of arson.

Craig was taken to the hospital for observation. In the morning he was discharged with sardonic compliments upon the thickness of his skull. He went to his desk in headquarters and sat down to write his report. It was nearly ten o'clock when one of the young women in the outer office came to where he sat.

"The Chief Marshal wants to see you at once," she said.

"How's the head?" asked the Marshal when he stood before the desk of his superior.

"Sore," Craig said with a grimace.

"Ready for duty?"

"Yes, sir."

"Describe what took place," the Chief Marshal ordered tersely.

"Priddy and I reported from Engine House Number One. We were ordered to go to the fire. When we arrived flames were coming from windows on the third and fifth floors. A red chief's car drove up and stopped in front of the jewelry store. Four men, one with a chief's helmet, got out and proceeded into the store."

"Didn't it strike you as odd that they should go into a place where there was no fire?" the Chief interrupted.

"It did, sir. But I thought it must be some special detail on account of the value of the stock-in-trade."

The Chief nodded. "What next?" he asked.

"The car was left running," Craig said with puckered brows. "Then Mr. Van Rensselaer was there and took my mind off it with questions and observations until the four men came out of the jewelry store. Two of them carried canvas bags. Somehow, sir, they did not look like firemen." Again he wrinkled his brows. "As a matter of fact, sir, they did not look like men at all."

"What do you mean by that?"

"It was their faces. I could see them plainly. They looked like the faces of wax dummies in a department store window. You know, sir. All pink and expressionless. The four faces were exactly alike. Then there was something about the car. I don't seem to remember what it was, but it will come to me."

"Go on," said the Chief.

"I knew, sir, that they must be stopped and asked to account for themselves, so I let out a yell to Priddy and made for them. . . . And that's the last I remember."

"They got clean away," said the Chief. "Clean away. Those four men and that car disappeared as if they had been erased. With their head start!"

"The jewelry store was looted, sir?"

"The swag will run into hundreds of thousands of dollars. The exact figures haven't been reported yet. The biggest robbery in the history of New York."

"The fires were incendiary, Chief?"

"No doubt of it. Crudely so. No effort made to conceal."

"Mr. Van Rensselaer said to hunt a motive," Craig said.

"Smart little man—if he is a double-dyed buff."

"The motive is pretty clear, sir, isn't it?"

"It doesn't belong in any of the usual categories," the Chief said. "Not for insurance; not for revenge, not a pyro. Not malicious mischief."

"But," suggested Craig, "to create a state of confusion that would make the looting of the jewelry store easy."

The Chief rumbled in his throat. He was an approachable man to the public and to his staff. He loved to talk but he never gabbled unwisely. It might create surprise that he discussed so important a matter with so new a subordinate, but it was his way, a part of his studied system to arouse initiative and create loyalty.

59

"There was plan and discipline and preparation," he said. "That red chief's car, now. That took time and foresight. Uniforms to be provided. Every move from arrival to getaway planned to the split second. Young man, it's my guess we're up against something new and bad."

"Like Mr. Van Rensselaer argues?" asked Craig.

"So he rode that hobby horse for you," said the Chief. "His flying squad of crooks. Here today and gone tomorrow. To a job in Chicago Thursday and Dallas Saturday. Lad, I'd hate to think it, but he has evidence on his side. . . . Well, the police have the organization and the men we lack. But all the same, it's our pigeon and we stick to it. Bear this in mind, my boy. We always work with the police, with no thought of jealousy. Mind you, now, I'll be in direct charge. But I'm detaching Priddy from all other duty to work on nothin' but this." He narrowed his eyes at Craig and there was a glint of humor in them. "And, since you're not yet good for anything else, I name ye to trail along with him." He snorted. "Maybe that phenomenal brain of yours'll find a use for itself. At any rate you'll be learnin'."

"Those masks!" Craig exclaimed.

"What about them?"

"Like Halloween," Craig said. "Rubber pullover masks."

"Now it may surprise you half to death, Batts," said the Chief ironically, "but some of us old-timers hit on that idea all by ourselves. . . . Be off with you. You'll be working with Priddy."

"Wait, sir," Craig said urgently. "I've remembered. Two things about that counterfeit chief's car. One thing—almost hidden under the back bumper was a hitch."

"A hitch? What in blazes is a hitch?"

"Like a coupling, sir. That car has been used to draw a trailer."

"And what else?"

"Red on the walls of the left rear tire. Red paint. That car was recently painted."

"So-oo," said the Chief Marshal.

"I would guess, sir, that there will be no use looking for a red car. If the crooks have a spot where they could paint it red, they'll go back there and repaint it some other color."

"About this hitch, now?"

"I would be thinking," Craig said, "that it points to a traveling

60

gang. Not local. That they came to town in a trailer and will ske-
daddle out of it again the same way. Moving on to their next job."

The Chief looked up with fierce blue eyes. His face was granite.
It did not soften as he came as close as he ever did come to paying a
compliment to one of his men.

"Keep figuring, Batts. It may be you'll turn out to be worth your
salt."

At the end of the day Craig went to the hospital to meet Nora
Fogarty. Nora had been permitted in her father's room before, but
this was the first time Craig had been permitted to accompany her.
The old Chief lay in his bed, head swathed in bandages. But his
gray eyes were bright and his distinguished Irish face smiling as
the young people entered. Nora bent over him to kiss his cheek.
He extended a firm hand to Craig and grinned a bit ruefully.

"You're right pretty in your tailor-made suit," he said. "How's
the fire marshal business? Boomin'?"

"Plenty of customers." Craig grinned. "We aim to give satisfaction. And you, Uncle Paddy, but for the swaddling clothes on your
noggin you look fit for duty."

"In a week I'll be out of here good as new. So give me all the
news. Until this day my head's ached so I'd no pleasure in readin' a
paper."

Craig provided all the department gossip and then gave the
elderly gentleman a detailed account of the jewelry robbery and of
his part in it.

"And this getaway car disappeared like it went down a rat hole,"
said Fogarty.

"North and east it went," Craig said. "It went to ground somewhere between Forty-second Street and Sixtieth. And between
Lexington and the river."

"It leaps to the eye," Fogarty declared.

"What leaps to the eye, Father?" Nora asked.

"That the fire where I got mine and the fire where you got
yours were set by a different class of people. Sure, my fire was set
for gain. For the insurance or some such purpose. Your fire was
set to cause a distraction and turn aside the eye. Them that set my
fire was retail torches; them that touched off yours was wholesale,
if ye get what I mean."

61

"Sure," Craig agreed. "Yours was local talent and mine nation-wide."

Chief Fogarty closed his eyes and leaned back against his pillow. He was tired. His lips moved as he repeated words that meant nothing to anybody but himself but which seemed to be the introduction to some old Irish fairy tale.

"Once upon a time," he said just above a whisper, "whin the r-r-rich was verry r-rich and the poor was ver-r-ry poor, there lived a lady wit' solid goold fingernails."

"We'd better go along, Craig," Nora said. "He's tired of us."

"There are many things I'm tired of," said the Chief, "and just now you're one of thim."

Nora kissed her father's forehead and then went quietly out of the room. "He'll be all right now," she said. "I've no more fear for him." Her brow puckered. "For the time," she said, "he seems to have forgotten what troubled him before."

"Not he," Craig contradicted. "It's that he's something else on his mind."

As they got off the elevator on the main floor of the hospital a huge box of flowers was being delivered. The girl at the desk, who knew Nora from her many visits to her father, called across to her, "Box of flowers for your father."

Nora, wondering who could have sent such an enormous bouquet to Chief Fogarty, walked across to the desk and examined the container. No information was visible except the florist's name and her father's. She puckered her arched brows. "Before it goes up," she said, "we will see whom it's from."

"Whom!" exclaimed Craig. "The girl's educated. Whom!"

"Open it," Nora snapped.

Craig cut the tape and lifted the cover. He estimated that someone had spent no less than fifty dollars for the contents. There was a small, white envelope which Nora opened. She read the enclosed card and passed it silently to Craig.

"Get well quick," it said. "There'll be a welcoming party," and the message was signed *Clyde Tupper*.

Craig slipped card and envelope in his pocket, and carefully tied up the cardboard box. The receptionist had not noticed his abstraction of the donor's greeting. "Send it along up," he said, and, taking Nora's arm, led her to the exit.

"It was best," he said, "to remove the stinger."

"Yes," Nora said. "It was a threat, wasn't it?"

"More like a warning and a reminder," Craig said.

"Craig," Nora asked, "what does this man do?"

"He has an office in a Broadway building. On the door it says 'Tupper Enterprises.' "

"What does that mean?"

He shook his head. "That we must find out," he said. "He makes money. And spends it."

"He knows someone doesn't like him," Nora said.

"You don't shoot people you're fond of," he answered.

"It was the way gangsters do," Nora said.

"Shooting out of a speeding car? It could be. It could be something else. In his case it could be a jealous husband or boy friend. He's a chaser."

He described to her the incident in the theater when Tupper had so brashly made advances to the delicious little chorus girl and had been assailed by her older sister.

"What show?" Nora asked.

Craig told her and she bobbed her head. "I thought so. That would be Annie and Fifi Mertz. I went to public school with them. Fifi was in primary. But even then she was a lovely little thing. If anyone looked at her crossways, Annie was at him tooth and nail."

"This Fifi child," Craig said, "was fresh out of a fairy tale."

"Keep your calloused, smoke-grimed hands off her," snapped Nora with sudden savagery.

"Hey, what gives?" expostulated Craig.

"Just a sisterly warning," she said, accenting the word sisterly. "A child as beautiful as Fifi, and as naïve, is as dangerous as a gas explosion in a basement."

"I'm unlikely ever to see her again. But if I do I'll wear a respirator."

"Never was there a mask invented," Nora said, still sharply, "to protect a softheaded man from a child like that. Not that's she's bad. From all I hear she's a sweet, modest, dumb child. But she'll

63

be like a typhoid carrier. When she walks abroad trouble takes her arm."

"What they call a *femme fatale?*" asked Craig ironically.

"Scraps and patches of education!" Nora said with a curl of the lip. "Next you'll be talking Latin."

"Which I can do," Craig boasted. "Like, for instance: *Timeo Danaos et dona ferentes.* Which being truly translated means, always look a gift horse in the mouth, especially if it's flowers from a Greek named Tupper."

"You're not on duty again till morning?" Nora asked.

"Right," he said. "We've the evening."

"For lack of a better man," she said, "I'll let you take me to dinner, and maybe to a movie."

He snorted. "Even when you were knee-high to a grasshopper you always wanted to tag along."

Her eyes flashed. "Craig Batts," she said, "did you ever take a look at me?"

"Why should I?" he asked carelessly.

"Tag along!" she said furiously.

"Like a coach dog under a fire engine," he grinned.

She stopped and stood facing him, chin up, shoulders back. "Then look me over now, numbskull. From top to toe, look me over. No longer am I knee-high to a grasshopper. Nor am I freckled nor spindly. You drool at sight of this Fifi Mertz. Well, there's many a desirable man drools at sight of me. Stand that girl beside me and I'll match her eye for eye, hair for hair, and, what's more important to you wolf-whistling weasel, leg for leg."

"Listen to the spittin' kitten," he jeered, but he did look at her as she stood there in the afternoon sunlight, and it was as if some veil had been removed from his eyes, or he were seeing her for the first time. It was a shock. Little Nora who had been a pest to be shaken off had changed into something quite different. She no longer was a kid to be sneaked away from, but a woman to lure. Fifi Mertz had a dazzling sort of beauty, a tempting beauty. Nora had a different, human, substantial beauty of the enduring sort—the kind that caught at the throat today, would be desirable in a ripened tomorrow; she was a woman to make men turn their heads in admiration even when the years rested lightly upon her.

64

Craig perversely would not let Nora see how she had affected him. Derisively he whistled.

"When your face and hands are washed, and your dress on straight, you're a neat-looking biddy," he said. "We will go uptown and I will feed you to cure the scrawny look of you."

CHAPTER NINE

THEY CAME to the surface in Times Square. Craig had intended to take Nora to dine in a pleasant little café on Forty-fourth Street. They walked northward and Craig paused at the somewhat grubby entrance to a six-story, faded brick building.

"This," he said, "is where Tupper holes up." He looked at his watch. "He won't be here at this time of day. Let's snoop a bit."

On the left-hand wall was a board on which the names of tenants were printed alphabetically. Tupper's office was on the fourth floor.

"So here we are," Nora said. "All right, Mr. Fire Marshal, what do we do? I'm simply swooning to see you be a detective." She grinned impishly up at him. "Go ahead and make my eyes pop."

"Results are brought by hard work, persistence and diligence," he said loftily, "rather than by genius or inspiration. And an intelligent approach. I will give you a sample."

He stepped to the cigar stand which faced the elevators and asked for cigarettes.

"Do you have theater tickets?" he asked.

"Next door in the basement," the man behind the counter said grumpily.

Craig leaned on the showcase. "I suppose you get to know most of the tenants in the building," he said chattily.

"So I get to know the tenants. So what of it?"

"Must be interesting," Craig speculated, "being here and getting to talk with so many different kinds of men. In odd businesses."

"What d'ya mean odd businesses?"

"Why, on the list I saw a company named Top Hole Novelty Company, and another they call Put and Take. Funny names."

"They got a right to pick what names they choose," said the cigar salesman.

"And I noticed one called Tupper Enterprises. Now what would that mean?"

"So," said the man, "you lead up to Tupper Enterprises. So it's Tupper Enterprises you're snoopin' around. What's the point, pally? You got a beef? Or are you a shamus, or what?"

"Just noticed the name."

"Sure, nosy. Now cast your eye over me. You'd say I was a healthy bozo, wouldn't you? Well, I don't keep that way by runnin' off at the mouth. Be on your way, pally, and take the moll with you."

Craig leaned confidentially on the case. "Too bad," he said sympathetically.

"What's too bad?" the salesman demanded.

"That you never will get far in the rackets. That you'll always be a punk."

"In the market for a thick ear?"

"Always," Craig said. "The reason you'll never make the grade is on account of you're not smart. Like you talk too much. You give things away. Like just now I drop a question about Tupper. So do you get smart and say he's in the insurance business, or he sells snails, or he's publicity man for a burleycue. Just casual. Not you. You got to show how tough you are and how you can't be pumped."

"Yah!" rasped the cigar counter man.

"And you give it away that your health might get poor if you talked about Tupper. Which tells me you think Tupper is tough and that his business won't bear talking about. No, friend, you'll never get farther than selling reefers or policy slips. Just a dumb cluck."

The elevator doors clanged open. The man looked over Craig's shoulder and his teeth showed in a malicious smirk. "Hey, Mr. Tupper," he called, "here's a nosy guy askin' questions."

Craig turned his back on the showcase and saw, ten feet away, Tupper standing in front of the elevator, and at his side was a girl. Craig's eyes opened a bit, for the girl was Annie's little sister, Fifi.

Tupper strode across the corridor, but stopped when he heard Nora exclaim, "Why, Fifi! So long since I've seen you!"

The child was frightened. Her lips parted and her cheeks paled. She tried hard to be casual but with little success. "Hello, Nora," she said shakily. "I—I—"

"Shut up," Tupper said roughly. And then, "Miss Fogarty." He turned to the cigar man. "So this character was asking questions?"

"And gittin' no answers," the man said.

With no warning, not even a narrowing of the eyes, Tupper's fist lashed out. Craig had been leaning against the showcase, his elbows behind him on the top surface. There was no time to interpose a guard, but in that split second he did duck his head so that the punch struck him on the forehead instead of the chin. Craig never had been struck a harder blow. Lightning seemed to flash. By sheer instinct he lowered his chin upon his chest and lunged blindly toward his assailant in an effort to clinch and hold on until his head could clear. Tupper, a sneer on his handsome face, stepped back a pace and lashed out, this time with a ready left fist. Craig went down, struggled to his knees as Tupper kicked him viciously on the shoulder so that he fell upon his face. The kick, aimed at his chin, had not found its mark. Tupper stood an instant enjoying himself. Then he reached for little Fifi's arm and jerked her around to face the street and led her away. The child uttered little bleating, terrified sounds.

Nora knelt beside Craig. He shook his head, got to his knees and arose shakily to his feet. The floor rocked under his feet and the building swayed before his eyes.

"Who's a dumb cluck?" asked the cigar salesman, licking his thick lips.

Oddly enough, Craig was unmarked. It was but seconds before fine condition and youth restored him to himself, except for a grinding humiliation that he had fared so ill under the eyes of Nora Fogarty. Nor did she spare him.

"The intelligent approach," she said tartly. "Any more samples to give?"

He grinned crookedly at her, but she saw the shame in his eyes. But he offered no excuses, gave no alibis. "He hits quick," was all he said, and in spite of his sudden defeat Nora felt inward pride in him for the way he took it. But she was careful not to permit him to see that pride or to sense that she was sympathetic. Craig stooped for his hat, settled it on his head and made no retort.

"Appetite spoiled?" he asked.

"It's famished I am," she said, pretending to be very Irish. "But can you gnaw soft bread with that jaw of yours?"

His quick mind veered away from his licking and from Nora's jeering. "That Fifi child," he said.

"Little idiot!" Nora said.

"She was frightened," Craig said.

"Little girls get frightened by men like that. But not frightened enough." Nora scowled darkly. "If harm comes to her, Sister Annie will not let it pass. This time the Tupper man should watch his step."

They moved away. The cigar salesman called after them, "When you want more information, just drop around."

Only one table was occupied in the little eating place which was their destination. They were seated and presently there was served to them a satisfying but not expensive dinner. For a time there was a certain stiffness between them, and conversation was not easy, but Nora was a girl who understood the meaning of tact and how to use it. She chattered about casual, unimportant things and presently Craig was chatting back, his dark mood dissipated.

"Nora," he asked seriously after their steaks were eaten, "did Uncle Paddy ever talk to you about the fire that killed my father?"

"Never. You know how close-mouthed Father is about department matters. Why do you ask?"

He shook his head. He shrugged. "Why," he asked, "do we go into it?"

"The department?" she asked.

"Yes. What's the attraction? Not money. A truck driver makes more. Maybe it's the uniform. A young lad may get a kick out of wearing the uniform. All right. He wears it, and barring promotions he gets to earn maybe five thousand, three hundred a year. After twenty years he retires on half pay. If he gets killed his widow, if any, gets a full year's salary and a pension of half pay. If I get injured so I'm no good, I get three-quarters' pay. . . . Now I'm not a numbskull. If I had gone into almost any other business, I could earn twice or three times as much, and maybe find opportunities to get rich." He frowned. "Did anybody ever see a rich fireman?"

"It's security," Nora answered. "There's many that set store by security. Come good times or bad times there's no worry about the job. No selling apples on street corners."

"But we get good men," Craig objected. "Not just coattail riders. It's not easy to get to be a fireman. We're a select body. So what are the rewards that attract us?"

"Thinking of resigning?" Nora asked.

"Suppose I were to resign. Suppose I go into some business and make money. Suppose I get all stirred up by ambition and end up with a million dollars and ulcers and a house on Fifth Avenue and an estate on Long Island. Is that better? Is it a better life? Do I get more pleasure or satisfaction out of it?"

"Why," Nora said, "that depends on the man. If he can be contented with a certain little, or if he's restless and pulled and hauled by wanting things, or if he's shoved by a dissatisfied wife who wants mink coats."

"Is lack of ambition a vice?" he asked more of himself than of Nora, but she gave an answer.

"There's good ambition and bad ambition," she said slowly. "There's the kind of ambition that's only selfish. That wants to get ahead simply to have power or money. I think that's bad ambition. Then there's the other kind, the kind that drives a man to accomplish, to do something valuable or distinguished. To such men money or power is not important when compared to contributing something valuable to the world. I don't see how the first kind could ever be happy. I don't see how the second kind could ever be miserable."

Craig considered that argument. "If you were a man, Nora, what would you want to be?"

"If I had the brains for it," she replied, "I'd wish to be a research scientist; a man whose whole ambition is to want to find out, whose life is concentrated on discovering something new in nature. He is engrossed. Money means nothing to him beyond supplying his modest needs. Power means nothing. He concentrates so hard that he's all but unconscious of the things that trouble ordinary men. He's serene. He's never bored and every day is an adventure. . . . Yes, that's what I'd like to be."

70

"That would be good," Craig said. "Very good. It would also be good to be a poet who cared for nothing but making words say beautiful things; or an artist who wanted only to make his colors and brushes bring into being a bit of beauty. Or a sculptor who could look at a block of marble and see loveliness in it and who had the skill of hand and eye to chip away the stone that concealed the beauty and make it visible to everybody."

"Yes," she said, "yes. Or a person who can think in sounds and arrange sounds so that they become a song or a symphony." She stared at the tablecloth. "It makes you reach the conclusion," she said softly, "that the finest accomplishments are those that create imponderable things, that create something that you can't touch or lift; and that the baser accomplishments deal in the fabricating of goods, wares and merchandise. I read in school about Sappho. Possibly nothing she wrote remains. But the mere fact that she did write beautiful songs makes her immortal."

Craig looked across the table at Nora and then grinned broadly. "My goodness!" he exclaimed. "How did we get into a wrangle like this?"

Nora wrinkled her exquisite nose. "Once in a while," she said briskly, "it's better to talk about the stars than about the sewers."

The mood departed, and perhaps both the young people were sorry for it—though the recollection of the fact that they had revealed something of their inner selves embarrassed them both to a point where flippancy became necessary.

"All the same," Craig said, "I'll bet Mike Angelo's mouth watered when he saw a pizza pie."

"How's for the Music Hall?" Nora asked. "Does your bank roll run to it?"

"Can just make it," he said, "if I ration myself for the next week."

So they went to the Music Hall and occupied comfortable seats in the mezzanine, and enjoyed the Rockettes and the stage show and the picture. When they came out at the end of the evening Craig proposed that they stop for flapjacks and coffee, but Nora vetoed and suggested scrambled eggs at home. Drowsily they rode the subway to Brooklyn and walked to the Fogartys' apartment a few blocks away from the entrance. They mounted the stairs and Nora opened the door. She clicked on the light and went through to the kitchen where she busied herself with eggs and coffee and toast. Craig sat on the kitchen table and watched and was contented.

"I'll always say," he told her, "that you look good over a hot stove."

"If you," she retorted, "had a heart, the way to it would be through your stomach."

The doorbell startled them. Nora, with that familiar gesture of all housewives, wiped her hands on her apron and went to the door. Craig scraped scrambled eggs from the skillet to their plates and then almost dropped the coffeepot as Nora screamed shrilly. He rushed through the dining room and living room to the little vestibule, where Nora stood, pale as death, staring down at the body of a man sprawled at her feet. He stirred and with what seemed a terrible effort raised his head and made gobbling sounds. Words were barely to be identified. Gurgle, cough. "Tell Chief. . . ." gurgle, retch. "Dutchman . . . tell. . . ." Then his head thumped to the rug and he lay still in death.

CHAPTER TEN

IT WAS Nora Fogarty's first contact with violent death, or with death in any form. She stood shivering with the shock of it, and somehow the most horrible part of it seemed to her the glistening bald skull of the man who lay at her feet. It seemed indecent. He lay, one arm under his body, the other flung outward as if grasping for something. She shrank back against Craig Batts, and he placed an arm about her shoulders. He drew her back into the parlor and pushed her down upon the davenport.

"If you're faint," he said, "put your head down on your knees."

"I don't faint," she said sharply.

"Sit there," he said, "while I telephone."

It was not the police he called for but the Bureau of Fire Investigation.

"Assistant Fire Marshal Batts here," he said. "I've got a murder on my hands. I'm at Chief Fogarty's apartment." He gave the address. "Will you notify the Chief? I'm calling the police."

Next he called the police. "I want to report a murder," he said. He gave the address, was told to remain where he was until the police arrived, and replaced the instrument on its cradle.

"Better look after the coffee," he said, thinking it well to give Nora occupation to distract her mind. But Chief Fogarty's daughter was not one whose mind needed distraction. She was pale but resolute.

"He was coming to see Father," she said.

"Right," Batts agreed.

"Coming," she went on, frowning, "to tell him something."

"Right," he repeated.

"And he was killed to stop him from talking."

"That," Craig said, "is how it looks."

He walked into the vestibule and, subduing a natural shrinking, bent over the prone body. That pallid, bald head affected him as it had affected Nora. He forced himself to feel for a pulse beat, but there was none. His eyes traveled from head to toe and came to rest upon the upflung hand. It was a surprising hand. The man had worn a soiled felt hat which now lay on the rug. His clothes were of cheap material, unpressed. Underneath the coat he wore a sweat-shirt. The trousers did not match the shirt, but, equally incongruous as were the hands, the feet were covered by silk socks of fine quality, and the shoes were of finest leather. Craig had seen their like in a Madison Avenue window and knew they must have cost no less than thirty-five dollars. But the hands! There was nothing rough about them. The nails were far from grimed or broken but polished and expertly trimmed. There had been a recent manicure.

There was almost no bleeding. The face, seen in profile, was that of a man in later middle age. Even in its awful stillness it seemed a well-nourished face. It was unshaven. Craig estimated a two days' stubble. From neck to ankles the man was a stumblebum. But feet, and hands, and ears and features belonged to a person of another class. Though the eyes were blank and dreadfully staring, Craig, taking them together with mouth and chin and nose, believed they had once displayed intelligence and possibly culture.

The man had been shot in the back—twice. Craig had heard no shots. The conclusion was either that the murderer had used a silencer or that the shooting had been done at some distance. How far, Craig wondered, could a man walk after suffering two such wounds? He had read of some extraordinary occurrences, of men walking incredible distances even when wounded unto death.

He wanted to go through the man's pockets, but decided against it. He would see what was there when the police made their search. This was police business, not on the surface at least fire marshal's business.

From the street came the screech of a siren, and in a moment two uniformed officers from a prowl car were tramping up the stairs. Craig stood to receive them. They stepped over the body into the vestibule. Craig forestalled their questioning. "I'm Assistant Fire Marshal Batts," he said, and displayed his identification. "Suppose we wait for the homicide men."

"They'll be here in two jerks," said one of the officers, and almost as he finished speaking there was the tearing scream of other sirens and within minutes the apartment was alive with officers in plain clothes and technicians of the homicide department.

Craig, with Nora close at his side, stood well out of the way in the living room. A dapper, slender, youngish man with olive complexion and brown liquid eyes, which could have had their origin nowhere but in Italy, detached himself from the group standing over the corpse and walked to them. He was not wearing his hat like some detective of fiction and he bowed in a mannerly way to Nora.

"You found the body, Mr.——?" he asked Craig.

"Assistant Fire Marshal Batts," Craig said.

"Lieutenant Fisano," the detective introduced himself.

"Miss Fogarty, daughter of Chief Fogarty," Craig volunteered.

The lieutenant acknowledged the presentation pleasantly.

"I did not find the body," Craig said in answer to the lieutenant's question. "It found us. Miss Fogarty and I were in the kitchen. The doorbell rang. Miss Fogarty answered and screamed. I went. The body, not yet dead, was sprawled upon the rug."

"So? . . . So. . . . Not dead?"

"He struggled to get up and gobbled words."

"Intelligible?"

"I could make out the words 'tell' and 'Chief' and 'Dutchman.'"

"That all?"

"Then he slumped down dead."

"Where," asked Fisano, "is Chief Fogarty? This is his apartment?"

"In the hospital. He was injured in a fire."

"But not *by* the fire," Fisano said. "Blunt instrument."

"Yes."

"Would you," asked Fisano, "say these two events were connected?"

"I have no reason for thinking so," Craig said cautiously.

"Did you hear shots?"

"None."

75

Fisano frowned. "One would say that the dead man came to see Chief Fogarty. To tell him something."

"Yes," agreed Craig.

"But there's a hitch," the detective said. "Newspapers and newscasts informed the public that Chief Fogarty had been assaulted and was in the hospital. It was a publicized fact. One naturally wonders why this corpus delicti didn't know it."

"It could be accounted for," Craig suggested.

"In what manner?"

"That he couldn't read and had no radio. That he had been absent from the city. That he had been in some position where news could not reach him."

"Such position as what?"

"Someone," Craig said, "didn't want him to wag his jaw to Chief Fogarty."

"Evident."

"Then his murderer must have known he had something to spill."

"So he must."

"Could a man guess that the murderer knew this for some time?"

"Conceivable," Fisano conceded.

"Even," Craig went on, "that he had been detained somewhere? Kept on ice."

"Any reason for thinking so?"

"Just a hunch."

"Hunches have some origin."

"Well," Craig said, "the corpse was out of his context."

"Meaning what?"

"Look him over, Lieutenant, and see if the rest of him fits his coat and pants."

"We'll talk more," Fisano said, and turned away abruptly. Craig saw him kneel beside the dead man and make a meticulous examination. A second officer in plain clothes came in from the corridor.

"Shot on outside," he said loud enough so that his words carried to Craig. "Blood on the stairs. Down the street. You wonder he could walk a step with two slugs in him there."

"I've seen strange things." He looked up as a sturdy figure stood peering through the doorway. "Hello, Marshal," he said. "I thought you might be along. Welcome to our city. You've a bright boy on the job."

"Young Batts, eh? Was he showin' off?"

The lieutenant shook his head. "A pair of eyes he's got," he said. "Things we might have missed if he hadn't called attention. Maybe it's not right, all men being equal under the Constitution. But it's human not to use as fine-toothed a comb on a fugitive from a bread line as it is on a respectable member of society."

"Would this, d'ye think, be any of the Bureau's business?" asked the Chief Marshal.

"I'd say you'd want to sit in," Fisano said, "and welcome as always."

"I'll talk to my bright boy," he said, and ambled across the room to the davenport where Nora sat with Craig standing at her side. He nodded curtly to Nora and narrowed his eyes at Craig.

"How come you here so promptly?" he demanded.

"He's like a member of the family, Marshal," said Nora. "He brought me home from seeing Father in the hospital."

"And how is the old smoke-eater?"

"About ready to be discharged," Nora said.

"Us from the auld sod are hard to kill," he said grimly. And then to Craig, "Tell," he ordered.

Succinctly and in dry official language Craig made his report. The Chief Marshal did not interrupt until he had finished. Then he said shrewdly, "And what are you holding back?"

Craig shook his head, and it was a stubborn gesture which his chief did not overlook. "My boy," the Marshal said, "if it has to do with Fogarty, then you're doing him no favor by hiding it. Is it that you have doubts of the integrity of the man that you fear to talk?"

"If," Nora said sharply, "if he doubted Father's honesty, he would be welcome in this house no longer."

"I would sooner doubt myself," Craig said. "Whatever it is he would sooner keep to himself."

"Then he has told you nothing?"

"Not a word."

"So you would be betraying no confidence," said the Marshal gravely. "Have you not yet learned that no honest man was ever harmed by the truth? But that to hold back the truth may bring grief to the innocent?"

77

Nora touched his arm, and her eyes smiled up at him with steady confidence. "The Marshal is right," she said.

"If that is your word," Craig said, but reluctantly. "Here it is, sir, all we know. For many days Uncle Paddy has been worried. Not like himself. His worry has to do with a man named Clyde Tupper, who comes at odd times and throws his weight about and has a sleek grin as if he had eaten the canary. When he comes Uncle Paddy sends us out of the apartment."

"Is that all?"

"I have seen him watching fires. Fires set by a torch."

"What is his business?" the Chief Marshal asked.

"It is in a cheap building on Broadway." He gave the address. "What his business is I tried to find out today. . . . He hits quick and hard." Craig's lopsided grin was rueful. He described his brief fracas with Tupper with truth and exactness.

"Is there any connection between that man and what happened here tonight?"

"Not that I can state," Craig said.

"You called Lieutenant Fisano's attention to discrepancies about the victim?"

"Yes, sir."

"He should have noted them himself."

"Probably he did," Craig answered.

"But you did not keep them to yourself—to tell me privately?"

"You, sir, impressed upon me that we work with the police."

"I give you a good mark," the Chief Marshal said, and Craig warmed to the words because this grim man was sparing with his commendations. "What did these discrepancies indicate?"

"That he was a man of means who could afford handmade shoes and costly socks and underwear. That he was a—a fastidious man whose hands were well kept and manicured. Shall I mention intangibles?"

"It is a ten-dollar word," said the Marshal. "If you know what it means."

"There was something about him, even in death and in that cheap, wrinkled suit, that made me think he was a cultured man. I might almost say an aristocratic man."

"You guessed that he had been held a prisoner?"

"Yes, sir."

78

"Is there an alternative to that?"

Craig nodded. "That he had been in hiding."

The Chief Marshal was puzzled. "If this man knew something—something about fires or about the department, why would he seek out Chief Fogarty and not me? I'm the one to handle such matters."

Craig shook his head. There could be but one reason, but he did not wish to express it. It was a deduction his superior was amply able to make himself. If the murdered man had come to Chief Fogarty instead of to the Bureau of Fire Investigation, it would be because Fogarty had some peculiar and personal connection with the affair which made it desirable to disclose whatever he came to tell to him instead of the Chief Marshal.

The Chief Marshal stood mute until the pause became awkward. Then, suddenly unbending, he clapped his hand on Craig's shoulder with a fatherly gesture.

"Here," he said, not at all harshly, but with sympathy and friendliness in his heavy voice, "is a deep and dark thing, and it will give anxiety and hard labor to all of us. But there is one point, Nora my girl, and young Batts, about which we need not be eating out our hearts. And that is the integrity of Chief Fogarty. Him I will guarantee. Whatever mess he is in, if there is a mess, it was not of his making, nor, when the truth is known, will it bring dishonor to him."

"Thank you, Chief," Nora said, and tears welled over her eyelids.

The police had left the apartment. The body had been taken in its basket to the morgue. It was very still, but a tension remained, a vibrating something which twanged the nerves.

"You are alone?" the Chief Marshal asked Nora. "Shall I send a man to keep his eye on you?"

"No need, Chief," Craig said. "I'll be staying."

For an instant the Chief Marshal frowned and looked sharply from face to face. But what he saw there made him smile gravely. Neither of these young people was aware that there was impropriety in Craig's staying the night alone with this girl—this beautiful and desirable girl. He cleared his throat noisily.

"Tomorrow will be another day," he said, and, turning his back abruptly, went down the stairs, accompanied by his ever-present aide, to the car that awaited him in the street.

CHAPTER ELEVEN

IT WAS the judgment of the medical officer that Chief Fogarty could with safety to himself be taken to the morgue to view the body of the man who had died in his apartment. He declined fiercely to be transported in an ambulance, but rode in his own car driven by his own aide. Craig Batts rode in the rear seat. They entered the gloomy building housing the unfortunate dead, and the body was brought into view from its niche. The Chief peered down at it long and carefully. Then he shook his grizzled head.

"Never before have I set eyes on the man," he said positively.

"Chief," asked Craig formally, "why should this man have come to you?"

"It makes no sense whatever," Fogarty said.

"Could there, sir, be a connection between this and the assault upon yourself?"

"There could," said Fogarty testily, "but what it is I'll not be guessing."

Craig drew this man, who stood to him in the position of a father, to one side and dared greatly with his next whispered question.

"Could there, Uncle Paddy," he asked, "be threads between this and whatever it is that is between you and that man Clyde Tupper?"

The Chief's face darkened and set like granite. "Whatever is betwixt him and me is private business and not to be pried into by any young spriggins."

"But, Uncle Paddy, none knows better than yourself that nothing that touches murder can be private business. And what man would be before you to declare that the truth harms none but the guilty?"

"Boy," said the veteran, "ye have scant experience of life or of the forces that can twist ye this way and that way. Nor, being young and self-righteous with the rigidity of youth, can ye perceive that a smaller evil thing may be pushed aside that a bigger badness shall be averted or a greater good be made to come."

"You're an older man and a wiser man and a better man than me," Craig said sadly, "but I think it is not the dumb stiffness of my youth that makes me maintain that no trucklin' with evil can ever give birth to good."

"We will speak of it no more," Fogarty said firmly but not angrily, and he rested his huge hand on Craig's shoulder. "The old age of a man would be happier could he cling to the ideals of his boyhood. . . . If he would never learn that all life is but a dickerin' with the devil in an effort to get the best of him at the end of it."

"What man," asked Craig gravely, "has the mother wit to play such a game of chess with Old Scratch?"

Chief Fogarty turned away. "I will go home now and get into my own bed, for I'm a tired man and not yet myself."

So they were sent to the Fogarty apartment where Nora was harsh with her father and drove him to his bed and came out of the bedroom to give Craig Batts a tongue-lashing for tempting her father to overexertion.

"It is not his body that is overtired but his mind that is overtroubled," Craig said.

"Whatever it is," she retorted, "not the President of the United States or even the Commissioner of the department gets in to see him till I give the word." It was but natural, coming from a line of firemen that stretched back into the old volunteer days, that she could give the Commissioner precedence over the President.

The Chief's car, at Fogarty's direction, took Craig down to headquarters. He occupied his desk adjoining that of Luke Priddy, who chose to be saturnine. "So," he said in his acid way, "you're working yourself into a new job."

"Meaning what job?" Craig asked, ready to take offense.

"Cease to bristle," Priddy said with a curling of the lip. "It's a job the like of which is not in the Commissioner's report."

"Such as?" Craig asked.

"Official catalyst."

"And what is a catalyst?"

"It's a thing that's cast among other chemicals and creates a reaction. Or maybe you're only a carrier like Typhoid Mary. Anyhow, where you set your foot trouble sprouts."

Craig grinned. "More likely I'm only the kid tied to the tree to lure the tiger."

"Maybe it's a gift. A handy gift for a marshal if it doesn't attract a lead slug in the belly or a sap to the noggin. . . . What do you make of all this? Commencing, we'll say, with the vanishing of the report on the fire that killed your father?"

Craig turned his head abruptly and eyed Priddy. "That," he said, "is supposed to be hush-hush."

"Friend of my childhood," Priddy said mockingly, "there's not a mother's son in this room that doesn't know the details. And don't ask me how. A little bird spread the news. If you could locate that little birdie, you might learn something to your advantage. 'A goodly apple rotten at the core,' as Mr. Shakespeare has it. Or, more aptly, in every barrel of apples there can be one rotten one."

"You wouldn't be able to point out that apple?"

"Not me," Priddy said, "but, to coin another witticism, I smell the odor of skunk."

Craig found he wanted to talk. He wanted to exchange thoughts. Always it cleared his head and made him reason more cogently if he could debate a question or even state it in words for himself to hear. It brought into action his subconscious mind, which he was only vaguely aware he possessed. But he did know through experience that there was some astonishing mental mechanism that was sharper and abler than conscious reasoning and that reached true conclusions by invisible paths. It cut corners and arrived at unexpected destinations. It seemed to work better, he had observed, if his objective mind became a vacuum—if he were in a state midway between sleep and awakeness. All at once, out of nowhere, came an answer or a solution, and without effort on his part. A sort of gift out of the infinite. Sometimes this sort of thing would pop out at him like a jack-in-the-box when it was least expected. But it was infallible when it spoke. It was a tap line into truth. He was learning bit by bit how to make it work; how to avail himself of its assistance. By experiment he had found that if he relaxed physically and forced extraneous matter from his mind, if he made his mind as nearly a blank as possible, then the message from the subconscious would come through, and his problem would be solved in a flash. It was as though there resided somewhere deep within him a reservoir of knowledge to be tapped easily if one but knew the method of it.

"It's odd," Priddy said, interrupting Craig's musings, "that the police haven't been able to make an identification of the body." He paused and thought about it. "But I imagine derelicts are difficult to identify. No place to start."

"But," said Craig, almost as a reflex and not by intention, "he was no derelict. Bathed and shaved he was, and carefully manicured. What's the word? *Fastidious*. That described him except for his hat and suit. His face makes me think of something." He sought to identify what it was those features resembled. Something aristocratic. Something ironically aristocratic. He was creeping up on it. It was almost within his grasp. And then it came to him. It was a comical picture in one of those supercilious magazines—a drawing of an old-time clubman sitting in the window of his club gazing half sleepily, half arrogantly out at the plebeian passers-by.

He stood up abruptly and went to the office of the Chief Marshal, who was able to receive him at once.

"Sir," he said, "may I have a copy of the police photograph of that dead man?"

"What do you want of it?"

"I want to try something, sir. May be a wild goose chase. At any rate, it'll do no harm."

The Chief called to his aide, directing him to get from the files a print of the photograph. It was an excellent, clear flashlight of the murdered man. Indeed there were three from different angles. They were placed in a large manila envelope and Craig went away with them.

"Why," asked the aide, "didn't you pin him down?"

"Sometimes," the Chief said, "it's a good idea to give a youngster rope. It sparks 'em."

Craig noted down a number of addresses from the telephone book and then took the subway northward. His first stop was at a famous club in the Forties where he showed the photographs to the doorman, but without success. He called at club after club with the same result until at last he came to one with a long and conservative history, whose membership were of the elite, and particularly of the aging elite. The imposing doorman was persuaded to look at the photographs, but his butler's inscrutable face revealed nothing.

"We are not permitted to give information about our members," he said firmly.

"So he is a member," Craig answered.

"I have not said so," answered the doorman.

"Then," Craig said, "you will take me to someone who has authority to give it out." He paused. "Of course I can take it up with the police. But I have police authority to subpoena."

"Please follow me," the doorman said, and led Craig to the office, where he displayed his credentials. "I wish to know," he said, "if this is a picture of one of your members."

The Secretary examined the pictures with shocked eyes. "This is a serious matter, Marshal," he said. "But there can be no object in making things difficult. I hope no disagreeable publicity for this institution will result."

"I see no reason why it should—if you are co-operative."

"I believe," the Secretary said, "that this is one of our members. But one hesitates to be positive. From a photograph—"

"Then," Craig said, "will you be so good as to go to the morgue with me?"

The Secretary shuddered with distaste. "I suppose I can't avoid it," he said reluctantly.

Craig felt justified in the expense of a taxicab which conveyed them downtown. The Secretary, as they approached their destination, grew pale and exhibited signs of panic. Craig reassured him.

"It takes but a second," he said. "It won't be bad."

Once inside and the attendant took them to the drawer in which were the remains of the murdered man. He uncovered the face. The Secretary opened his eyes and looked and staggered as if about to faint. He closed his eyes again, and Craig steadied him with a firm hand.

"Well?" he asked.

"It's him," said the Secretary faintly, careless of his grammar. "Get me out into the air."

Craig led him to the street before asking further questions, and hailed a taxicab. "I—I could use a drink," the Secretary said.

"Stop at the first bar," Craig directed, and there, while the dapper Secretary fortified himself with a stiff whiskey, Craig was content with a small beer.

"All right now?" he asked presently.

"All right."

"Fine. . . . What's his name?"

"Mr. Williamson Tecumseh Peabody."

"A member of your club?"

"A very old and honored member."

"His address?"

"I would have to look in the book."

"His occupation?"

"Mr. Peabody had no occupation. What I mean is that he was a man of means. His family has possessed wealth and distinction for generations."

"Was he eccentric?"

"On the contrary, he was one of the most dignified and conservative of men."

"Who," asked Craig, "were his intimate friends—his cronies—in the club?"

"Now that is a difficult question," the Secretary answered. "He was a reserved man, courteous and considerate. But he played neither bridge nor other games. It was his custom to lunch alone at a small table. His habits were fixed. He arrived in the club daily at twelve o'clock; went to the library, where he examined the newly arrived periodicals. At one o'clock precisely he went to his table in the dining room. After luncheon he always went to the lounge and occupied a chair where he sat and dozed and looked out at the avenue."

"Sort of a lone wolf?" Craig said.

"You couldn't say that. He was not offish. If a member spoke to him, he would chat. He attended the functions of the club. He simply was—as I have told you—reserved. Possibly shy."

"Would any of the club servants know more about him?"

85

"I fancy not. He invariably treated them with consideration and was generous at the time of the Christmas funds. He knew them all by name. But I doubt if he ever exchanged half a dozen words with any of them."

"Sort of an eccentric?"

"I would not say so—no more so than dozens of our members. Gentlemen, when they reach a certain age, especially if they have wealth and family, are entitled to their small peculiarities. What in—ah—more commonplace people might be termed oddities, in our members are only amiable characteristics."

"It all depends," Craig said with straight face, "upon what block you live in and whether your great-grandfather smuggled rum or owned a slaver or had dealings with Blackbeard the pirate."

"Many of our gentlemen," the Secretary said imperturbably, "have a just pride in their ancestry and family histories."

Craig reflected that his inspiration had led him into a stream where he might well find himself beyond his depth. He well knew that such things as influence existed. He had come into contact with political influence of a sort; but there was a more insidious influence which rarely became visible. It was none the less potent. He knew that in a time of stress there could be a rallying around, a mysterious exertion in behalf of. One could not, especially one of Craig's years and experience, put one's finger on its source. But when trouble involved such an individual as William Tecumseh Peabody, it was best for assistant fire marshals to take to cyclone cellars. Peabody probably was connected by blood or marriage or long family association with two-thirds of Fifth Avenue and the aristocracy of Long Island and Westchester. Their connections would ramify to San Francisco and Detroit and the Senate and embassies in Washington.

Craig, very wisely, decided that he had gone as far as would be clement for himself, and that he had better enlist for himself powerful reinforcements.

He thanked the Secretary and indulged himself in the improper expense of a taxi back to headquarters. He took the elevator up to the eleventh floor and opened the door of the Chief Marshal's reception room. The Chief's aide looked up from his book.

"Now what?" he asked.

"Will you tell the Chief it's urgent?" Craig said.

"He's alone. You can go in," the aide said.

The Chief Marshal scowled at the interruption. The speaker on the desk chattered. Bells pinged. Outside the window lower Manhattan with its massive structures spread about them—a mighty city. A most puissant portion of a mighty city. The sight of it somehow daunted Craig. The thought that he was a servant of this enormous mass of brick and granite and iron with a duty to aid in preserving it from harm—of preserving it and what it represented from evil forces—made him feel tiny, insignificant, absurdly wee and insanely vain to think he could even help to cope with so monstrous an entity. Millions of human beings; billions of dollars of vulnerable wealth!

"Well," demanded the Chief harshly. "Out with it."

"I've identified him, Chief," Craig said.

"Identified who?"

In the stress of the moment he became human and not official. "The corpse up at Uncle Paddy's," he said.

"Who was he, and how did you make identification?"

"It was a sort of a hunch, sir," Craig said, "that started with a funny picture in a magazine."

"There are days," said the Chief, "that are worse than other days. So now comes to vex me a boy that's daft."

Craig hesitantly described to his superior the train of thought that had led him from a printed picture to the name of a dead man. The Chief Marshal listened with no change of expression on his formidable face.

"Like that, was it?" he said at the end. "You should quit the department and buy a crystal ball. Don't boast of this thing or you'll get an ill reputation for being unchancy. . . . And what was his name? What was the name of him?"

"His name," said Craig, "was William Tecumseh Peabody. With a house on Fifth Avenue facing the Park. And there's no great family in the city that he's not just like that with." He held out two fingers pressed together.

The Chief's face went blank. "Ye stuck in your thumb and you pulled out a plum," he said bitterly, "and the plum's too hot for me to handle. So we'll pick it up with tongs and lay it on the desk of the Commissioner. . . . Bad luck to the day I was bamboozled by your tricks. We will now be the bearers of disturbing news."

He arose and, followed by Craig, strode down the corridor, turned to the right and thrust open the door of the Commissioner's reception room.

CHAPTER TWELVE

IT WAS not without trepidation that Craig Batts entered the Commissioner's office, but any feeling of unease was quickly dissipated by the man who headed the department.

"Something urgent?" he asked the Chief Marshal.

"This lad," was the reply, "has dug up the identity of the man that died in Fogarty's apartment."

"Excellent," said the Commissioner, appraising Batts with keen eyes.

"Excellent it was, what with his trick mind. But I could wish the police had done it."

The Commissioner passed over the wish about the police and fixed his attention on the trick mind. "What kind of a mind?" he asked.

"One that makes queer leaps to right conclusions," said the Chief Marshal, and explained to the Commissioner the observations and reasoning which had led Craig to his goal. The Commissioner nodded and peered more closely at Craig. He nodded again. "It was well done," he said, and glowed at this praise from so exalted a quarter.

"Now what about the police?" the Commissioner asked.

"Because it could be too hot to handle, and I wish it was their baby. The corpse's name is William Tecumseh Peabody."

"What!" exclaimed the Commissioner.

"The identification is certain, sir."

"And you don't like it?"

The Chief Marshal stood mute. The Commissioner's fine eyes flashed. "Is it influence you are afraid of?" he asked.

"No sensible man likes to stand on the tracks with an express train bearing down on him."

"I'll handle that phase of it," snapped the Commissioner. "If influence meddles it'll get a bloody nose." He paused with half-shut eyes. "This," he said, "will be duck soup for the tabloids."

"Even the *Times*," the Chief Marshal responded ironically, "may mention it on page three."

"Have you notified the police?"

"I came straight to you."

The Commissioner lifted the telephone from its cradle and spoke into the mouthpiece. "Get me the Police Commissioner," he said. "Tell his secretary I'm calling and it's urgent."

He waited and presently spoke again. "The same to you," he said in response to what must have been a courteous greeting. "Something has broken. Can I come over immediately? . . . Right. I'm on my way."

He turned back to the Chief Marshal and Craig. "Murder," he said, "is police business, not ours. But this one seems to touch the department. So we'll hold a watching brief. I'll take it from here." He narrowed his eyes at Batts. "You are to be commended," he said.

Craig followed his superior out of the office and, in the corridor, the older man growled *sotto voce*, "If it was a derelict in a bum's lodginghouse, Commissioner wouldn't be visiting Commissioner."

Craig was not displeased with himself. But for him it was possible that William Tecumseh Peabody might have gone to his rest in a pauper's grave. Then he reflected that, all things considered, it might have been just as well if the gentleman had done so. There would have been no furore and hullabaloo in the papers and over the air. There might not have been the complications, social and political, that were sure to ensue. However, so far as Craig Batts was concerned, there would be a credit mark on the records.

It was a day of drudgery for Craig. His assignment to the incendiary fire which had made possible the jewel robbery had been interrupted by the murder in Chief Fogarty's neighborhood. That, now, was in the hands of the police. The robbery had been perpetrated by men in firemen's uniforms. That was a lead. Those uniforms came from someplace. The most likely source was some costumer's. So Craig was ordered to canvass such establishments in an effort to locate the one from which the uniforms had been hired.

He trudged from place to place in Manhattan, displaying his credentials and asking questions. Before nightfall he had covered almost every one in the city and looked forward to a toilsome to-morrow repeating the search in Brooklyn.

No costumer could be located who had rented four uniforms including a chief's helmet within recent weeks. But in a dingy, cluttered store in the Forties he encountered a talkative clerk who volunteered information that, on the face of it, was useless.

"Haven't rented a fireman's uniform in months," said the young man. "Soldiers' uniforms—yes. Salvation Army—yes. Last one we rented was cops' uniforms. Masquerade party on Long Island. Yeah. Four cop suits, one of 'em a lieutenant's."

"Been returned yet?" Craig asked idly, not greatly interested.

"No," the clerk answered. "Hardly due yet. Lemme remember. . . . Party was last night."

"Rent any other suits for the same party?" Craig asked, more or less as a routine question.

"No. Kind of funny, ain't it? You'd think—"

Craig found himself suddenly interested. He asked where the party was held. He was given the name of the man who had hired the uniforms. The party was held, so the clerk informed him, on the estate of Timothy Dodge in Roslyn.

Craig chatted amiably for a few moments and, asking to use the telephone, reported in and advised that he was on his way home. He took the subway to Brooklyn and in less than an hour arrived at his apartment. Something was nagging at his mind. Something was demanding to be done. He was conscious of discomfort, and the discomfort involved those four policemen's uniforms rented for the Long Island party. Besides having a trick mind, he had a mind that had profited by training. One point that had been impressed upon him was to follow up every lead, important or insignificant. To pry into anything that attracted his attention or excited his curiosity.

He went to his telephone book and looked up the number of the Dodge estate in Roslyn. Then he lifted the instrument and made the call. A man's voice answered presently.

"Is this the residence," he asked, "of Mr. Timothy Dodge?"

"It is."

"May I speak with Mr. Dodge, please?"

"Mr. Dodge is in Europe."

"When did he go?" Craig asked, his interest quickening.

"Who is speaking, may I ask?" the voice inquired.

"Assistant Fire Marshal Batts," Craig said. "Who are you?"

"I am Mr. Dodge's butler," said the man. "Fire Marshal, you say?"

"Yes."

"Is something wrong, sir? I mean if there is, then you should call Mr. Dodge's attorneys."

"Nothing like that," Craig assured him. "I merely wished to ask if there was a party at your house last night—a large costume party."

"Indeed not, sir. None of the family is in residence. Most certainly there was no entertainment of any character here last night—nor for two months past, owing to the absence of the family abroad."

"Was there such a party in the neighborhood, do you know?"

"I'm sure I should know if such a merrymaking had taken place. Some word of it would have reached me, I am sure. Nothing of the sort in this vicinity."

"I'm obliged," Craig said, and replaced the instrument on its carriage.

No costume party on the estate of Timothy Dodge! None in the neighborhood! Four policemen's uniforms had been hired under false pretenses! He sat down in his comfortable armchair and closed his eyes.

Four uniforms, he thought. The same number as had been made use of in the jewel robbery. Could it be he had hit upon a method? Criminals, he had been taught, were creatures of method. A firebug, for instance, would use over and over again the same device. A safecracker's work could be identified as if he had set his signature to it. Was it possible that here was another such signature? An expert can identify the painter of a picture, if unsigned, by the character of his brush strokes. Four uniformed men. Four municipal employees. The first four were firemen; the second four were policemen. Only a slight variant.

There was something else to think about; something to add to this line of reasoning. It was the repeated assertion of Pieter Van Rensselaer of his suspicions that an organized gang was operating in the country. The dapper little buff was obsessed by the idea that there was a mobile organization of criminals pouncing now in San Francisco, now in New Orleans, now in New York. Certainly the men who had robbed the jewelry store had made use of a trailer.

Taking all this into consideration, Craig reasoned—setting out all the facts in line—it was not fantastic to deduce that a new depredation might be planned, using a police squad car instead of a red fire department machine. But this new raid, if the reasoning were correct and if Van Rensselaer were not utterly mistaken, would not occur in New York. It would be in some distant city to which the criminals would be transported in their trailer. If the whole thing were not a mare's nest, then word would come presently of an incendiary fire in some distant city and a raid upon a bank or a jewelry store or a fur warehouse under cover of the excitement and turmoil—a raid by four men disguised as policemen.

The longer Craig thought about the thing, the more firmly convinced he became that he was right. But even if his reasoning were correct, it was of little practical use. Even if it were true that he had detected a method, he had no idea where that method would be applied. There was every sizable city in the United States to choose from. There was no conceivable way in which to issue a warning.

The telephone seemed to explode in his ear. The sound of it was startling, so deep was he in his problem. He shook his head, closed his eyes in irritation and reached for the receiver. It was Nora's voice.

"Craig," she said, "there's trouble."

"What kind of trouble, Cupcake?"

Her voice was almost shrill, which was not its custom. It was usually so soft, so restrained, so musical. "Father," she said, "is gone. And Fifi Mertz is here."

This was a combination of events without rhyme or reason. But they could not be reconciled over the telephone. He wasted no words.

"Coming," he said, and hung up the instrument.

He thrust on his hat and sped down the stairs. He could reach the Fogartys' apartment in five minutes afoot. He walked at speed and reached the apartment in four. He ran up the stairs and pounded on the door. It was opened instantly by Nora. He could hear sobbing from the living room.

"What gives?" he demanded.

"I was out at the store. Father was sitting in his robe and slippers. When I came home, he was gone."

"Left no word?" Craig tapped his head. "Was he all right here?" he asked.

"They wouldn't have let him come home otherwise," she said. "He was reading his paper, and mad at the Republicans." She compressed her lovely lips. "I ran down to the street. Some boys playing in front saw him go. Uniform cap and badge and all. He got in a car. Cadillac convertible, they said. A man driving." She paused. "They said the man's head was bare and his hair stood on end."

"Tupper," Craig said, and she nodded.

"Now the Mertz kid," he prompted. "Why is she here?"

"She's frightened to death. She was alone. Poor kid thought I could do something."

"About what?"

"Sister Annie," Nora said. "Sister Annie is loose on the town with Mr. Mertz's police positive."

Craig brushed past Nora and stood over the dainty child who crouched on the davenport sobbing convulsively. She was far from fairylike now.

"Stop your noise," Craig said peremptorily. "What goes on?"

"Annie. . . . Annie. . . . She found out. Papa and Mamma . . . away."

"It's Mertz's day off," Nora said. "He's a policeman."

"I know," Craig said. "So Annie found out?"

"I didn't do anything wrong. I didn't. . . . I didn't. Just went out with him. With Tupper."

"So," Craig said, "Sister Annie blew her top." He jerked his head. "She does just that," he said to Nora.

"She—she slapped me. And then she took Papa's gun and ran out. And she'll shoot him. . . . She'll kill him."

"Not a bad idea," Craig said grimly. "Listen, you," he said to Fifi. "Sit right where you are. Don't move. We'll go see. Where does Tupper live?"

"In—in that building. There's a bedroom—a room fixed for a bedroom—"

"Right," said Craig.

94

"I'm coming," Nora said. "Maybe he took Father there."

"Stay with the kid," he said.

"No."

He knew well that when she used that tone there was no use to argue.

"Then stir your stumps," he ordered. "Subway'll be quickest."

The time seemed interminable as they rumbled through Brooklyn and under the river. At last they emerged at Times Square and almost ran to the building in which Tupper lived and carried on his business. The cigar stand was closed for the night. Craig and Nora took the elevator upward and got off at Tupper's floor. His door was to the left. Annie Mertz stood before it kicking it and pounding.

"Open up. . . ." she screamed. "Open up and get what's coming to you. . . ."

Craig started to run. Tupper's door opened and the man stood there scowling. Annie pointed the gun with both small hands. Craig left his feet in a diving tackle, and as his arms closed around her legs the gun went off in his ear. . . . He had thrown the girl a dozen feet and she lay prone. The gun skidded along the floor. He was stunned by the shock of his lunge and collision with the floor. As he struggled to his knees he heard Nora's voice.

"Father . . . Father. . . ." she cried.

CHAPTER THIRTEEN

CRAIG, shaken, bruised, skin of his elbows abraded, pushed himself to his knees. Annie had bumped her head and lay prone and motionless. More or less by reflex action Craig scrambled to the revolver with which the girl had meant to shoot Tupper, and only then did he get to his feet to see Nora standing in the door, her arms about her father's waist and her face buried in his coat. Tupper was sardonic as he surveyed the scene.

"Should I be grateful to you, Batts, for saving my life?" he asked.

"That," Batts answered shortly, "wasn't the intention."

"No?"

"It was to save a hysterical girl from committing a murder." He paused and narrowed his eyes at the man in the door. "Of which I might personally approve," he added.

Craig picked up the still-unconscious chorus girl in his arms.

"Hadn't we better move this circus inside," asked Craig, "before the neighbors get inquisitive?"

"The neighbors don't get inquisitive," said Tupper bleakly. But he stood aside, as did the Fogartys, to let Craig carry the girl inside. They were in a reception room which gave into an office. Beyond the office, through an open door, could be seen living quarters. Craig carried Annie to the bedroom and laid her upon the bed.

"Make yourself at home," Tupper said.

It was a complete apartment behind the offices—bedroom, kitchenette, living room with dining alcove and bath. It had cost money to convert the space to its present uses, and it had cost more money to furnish it as Tupper had done. There was surprising good taste and comfort. The rug on the living-room floor was Aubusson. On the walls were excellent prints. There were two handsome Chippendale armchairs, though Craig could not have identified them. In a corner was an ancient olivewood Spanish vargueno inlaid with ivory. There was an overstuffed davenport and deep, soft chairs. The whole was luxurious, costly. Without meaning consciously to do so, Craig memorized the contents.

"Better take a look at the kid," he said to Nora, who went into the bedroom.

"Can I serve refreshments?" Tupper asked ironically.

Chief Fogarty had not spoken. Now he sat collapsed in a chair in Tupper's office, ghastly pale, hands trembling. The shock of what had gone on under his eyes had been too much for him—so freshly released from the hospital.

"I think he could use a drink," Craig said. "Then I'll get him home to bed."

"Perhaps," Tupper said, "the Chief doesn't want to go home to bed. Maybe he wants to finish our conversation."

"That's for him to say," Craig told the man with bristling hair.

He did, however, provide a glass of whiskey for the Chief, who gulped it and appeared to be benefited. He sat erect now and glowered at Craig.

"I will not be followed and spied upon," he said harshly.

"It was not you, Uncle Paddy, that brought us here, but the Mertz girl with her father's gun. It would not be fit for me to meddle with your private business, though it was with the devil himself."

"Then be on your way."

"There's Nora and the Mertz girl," Craig said.

Tupper walked around his desk and sat in his swivel chair. Craig leaned against the wall. There was silence in the room as they waited.

To Craig's eyes as he stood there peering about the room there was nothing to indicate Tupper's business. His desk was neat. No papers littered its top. There was a blotter, an inkwell, a tray for pencils and a holder for a pen. That was all. The rest of the office disclosed no more. It contained a filing cabinet and a bookcase which held only a few volumes. There was one book, not strictly a book but many pages secured in a binder, that Craig's eye recognized with surprise. It was a thing not too readily to be obtained by the public. It was the Code of Regulations for the Uniformed Force of the Fire Department of the City of New York.

Whatever business Tupper pursued it seemed to be lucrative, and it required no employees, not even a secretary. That made it a very personal concern; perhaps confidential. There were no signs of ledger or journal or other bookkeeping equipment. But there must be records. The Internal Revenue Department being what it was, every citizen who earned a dollar must put that fact down on paper somewhere or the income tax people would regard it with suspicion. There was a telephone but no typewriter was visible.

"You," said Craig, "should be on that television program."

"Indeed? Which one?"

"Where the panel guesses what your business is," Craig said.

"I'd baffle them," Tupper said with a shrug. "But I'll give you a hint: I'm self-employed."

"Is there a product involved? Or do you deal in services?"

"Oh, in services definitely." His eyes narrowed. "I operate an exterminator service. I eradicate pests. You are rapidly coming under that head, Batts."

Nora came into the office. She did not look at Tupper and spared only a brief, questioning glance for Craig. She rested a slender hand upon her father's shoulder in a caressing, reassuring way.

"I think we can take the Mertz girl home now," she said in an unyielding voice. Then an impish grin lightened her face. "She's going to have the granddaddy of all shiners," she chuckled. "You're rough with your lady friends, Craig."

"She's no lady friend of mine," he snapped. "I'd as soon cuddle a stick of dynamite."

There was a flurry and Annie Mertz swirled into the room. The side of her pert face was abraded where it had struck the floor and there was already visible the commencement of a black eye which would keep her out of the chorus line for days. She eluded Nora's grasping hands and, little hands turned into claws, she launched herself at Tupper where he sat. Her red nails raked his cheek. Craig made no move to stop her but stood ready to intervene if Tupper defended himself too roughly.

98

Annie was screaming hysterically; uttering shrill, incoherent words which displayed no mean vocabulary of invective.

"I'd have killed you. . . . I'd have shot you. But quick killing is too good for you." She hurled epithets at the man which astonished Craig, who had at his command no mean vocabulary of his own. Tupper fended her off; grasped her arms above the elbows. She kicked at him furiously.

"Hold her off me before I have to hurt her," Tupper spluttered.

Craig lifted her, kicking, in his arms and held her helpless.

"That's a sufficient plenty, Pepper Pot. You've prettied him up enough. . . . And give thanks, ye little vixen, I was here to stop you from doing worse."

Suddenly she was inert. She threw her arms about Craig's neck and buried her face under his chin and sobbed convulsively.

"Hey," he appealed to Nora. "Take her off of me. Like a limpet she is. Unloose me." But Nora did not move to his rescue. The little Mertz girl, one arm still around Craig's neck, lifted her head and turned her face toward Tupper. Hysteria was gone, and in its place was cold venom. . . . Cold and calculating venom.

"Tupper," she said almost in a whisper, "for what you've done I'll make you suffer. Maybe I'll kill you. But I'll put the fear of it on you. Never, by day or by night, will you know if I'm somewhere near. You'll not hide from me." Great, gasping breaths choked her for an instant. There was something about her that was impressive, that made one hold one's breath. When she continued to speak again it seemed to be with clairvoyance. "There is something that you fear to have known. I will find it out. I'll be your shadow that you cannot rid yourself of. . . . Mind what I say, Tupper. I do not think I shall kill you; but I'll pull you down and see that you come to a horrid end." She stopped speaking, and then said to Craig, "Put me down now, Mr. Batts. I will do no more this day. . . . But you, Tupper, in sunlight and in darkness, keep looking over your shoulder. I'll be close behind you."

It was melodramatic with the sort of melodrama people of her class are capable of achieving. Somehow, in that moment, in that room, it did not seem absurd. Certainly it did not seem laughable. She spoke what she felt in the only words she could use to express her meaning, and not a soul in that office but knew she uttered no idle threats. And so, for seconds, each person stood motionless

99

staring at Tupper. And it was to be seen that the man's cheeks grew pale, and that his eyes shifted to right and to left to hide the fear that was in them.

Then he laughed, not sincerely but artificially, and shrugged his shoulders.

"Will it be convenient if I have the use of my office now?" he asked.

Strangely it was Chief Fogarty who spoke in his deep voice with its touch of brogue.

"Sure, Tupper, ye may have the use and benefit of your office, and much good may it do ye. From now on a black thing will be riding your shoulders, as ye have made a black thing to ride mine. We will see which can throw it off. . . . Come, one and all." His voice in that final command was full and strong.

They descended to the street and Craig hailed a cab to carry them to the Fogarty apartment. Fifi was still there, big-eyed and tearful. Annie ran to her and enfolded the child in her arms.

"But I didn't. . . . I didn't. . . . It's not true. . . . I'm still a good girl," she whispered brokenly.

"Maybe so. No credit to him. We will now go home, and never again will you show what you've got in the chorus line to wet-lipped men."

"Your father's gun," Craig said. "What to do with it, he being a cop?"

"It will be safe with me, Mr. Batts," Annie said. "I will put it back where it belongs." And then she looked at him with level eyes and nodded her shapely head. "I'm obliged to you, Mr. Batts." And then to Nora, "You've got yourself a good man. Hang onto him."

To this Nora made no reply save to flush.

"I will see you home," Craig said.

"No need," Annie said. "This day can hold no more. We will be safe."

Chief Fogarty, when the girls had closed the door behind them, looked up from his chair. "Me bed calls for me," he said in a voice that tugged at their hearts. "It's bone weary I am. I would be alone and sleep."

He stumbled as Nora steadied him to his bedroom door. "Is there nothing you want to tell us, Father?" she asked softly.

"It would be the three of us against the world," said Craig.

"It is a thing," the Chief said, his voice robust for an instant, "that nobody can carry but me. . . . And I will carry it."

He closed the door and left the young people staring into each other's eyes.

"Poor, lonely Dad," said Nora softly.

"I must call headquarters and report in," Craig said.

"Then you will stay for supper?"

"And much obliged to you."

He used the telephone and then went down to the corner newsstand for an evening paper. He sat down on the davenport to read while Nora busied herself in the kitchen. There was the usual foreign news of ill-omen on the front page and the evidence in a congressional investigation. In a box at the bottom of the page under a Cleveland dateline was a story that made Craig sit erect with excited interest. It was the account of a bank robbery in the city on Lake Erie. It was a daring, daylight depredation, executed under cover of a three-alarm fire in an adjoining building. The looting had been done by uniformed men who drove to the door in an armored truck such as is used for the transference of cash or currency of bullion to some destination. The guards in charge of the armored vehicle had held up the bank and escaped with their plunder before the alarm could be given.

It was a repetition of the depredation in which Craig had played so unsatisfactory a part—a repetition with skillful variation. Here was more and conclusive evidence that Pieter Van Rensselaer was right in his deduction that an organized gang was operating according to schedule and plan in widely separated cities throughout the United States.

The telephone rang stridently and Craig lifted the receiver.

"Assistant Marshal Batts?" asked a voice.

"Yes."

The voice gave an address on the lower East Side in the congested loft district. "Get there on the run," ordered the voice. "Looks like it's our dish of ham and eggs."

Craig went to the kitchen door. "Got to get on the job," he said.

"Cup of coffee first?"

"No time," he told her. "Shall I come back here tonight, or can you hold the fort?"

"All that good food going to waste," she said thriftily. "Don't worry about Dad and me."

CHAPTER FOURTEEN

THIS FIRE was no amateur effort. The indications pointed to a skilled professional. It was no clumsy gasoline fire, but when Craig went in behind the protective water curtain thrown before him by the fog nozzle he found that the blaze had been timed by a candle, one of the sort that burned forty-five minutes to the inch, and that the inflammable substance had been celluloid. Suspicion was immediate that the motive was to collect insurance. But Craig, as he examined the box of a safe, became convinced the insurance was not all. When the heat abated an expert was called in who managed to open the safe and found its contents either burned to ashes or charred to illegibility. The records of the business had been destroyed, and the reason must be either to abolish records of a fraudulent nature, or figures that might lead to conviction of federal tax evasion.

Craig, in the dank, charred office, faced the proprietor of the business, who was a very frightened man who was not difficult to break. He was speedily reduced to stammering tears.

"They said—they guaranteed—it couldn't be found out," he chattered. "It was—it was a guarantee."

"You don't say!" Craig exclaimed sympathetically. "So you relied on them and they did a flop." He was excited. He was on the track of something important. Repeatedly it had been asserted in newspaper interviews that there was no commercial arson in the city. The boast had been that this form of crime had been eradicated. In times of prosperity, such as existed at present, there was much less reason for it than in days of depression. This did not mean that there was not the ever-present threat of arson by men whose businesses did not prosper, or by individuals with fraud to conceal, or whose tax returns had been dishonestly made. But the belief was that there was not a sufficient field for professional arsonists. The confession of this man made it appear that this condition did not exist, and that there was a man or an organization of men who were prepared to apply the torch on a salary or commission basis.

"So," Craig asked in his friendliest voice, "you didn't set this fire yourself?"

"I wouldn't know how."

"So you hired these people to do the job?"

"That's it, Marshal. That's how it was."

"But," Craig asked, "how did you know where to find someone who would strike the match?"

"It was a letter. And then I inquired around and—and different ones said they were reliable."

"You mean these arsonists actually circularized?"

"Sure. Oh, sure."

"With a name?"

"They called themselves A Friend in Need. They said something about if business was bad and creditors made trouble, to get in touch with them. Or if you needed money quick. Or if there were tax troubles. Or if you had insurance problems. Like that. Hinting."

"But they surely didn't give an address."

"Not like an office or a street number. Just said that their Mr. Brown would telephone for an appointment."

"How did they know you would be in the market for their services?"

"Such news like a man's got financial troubles, or like that, gets around among the trade."

"Right. And their Mr. Brown did telephone you?"

"Yes."

"And made an engagement?"

"Sure."

"Where?"

"On a street corner."

Craig nodded. That's the way it would be. "And at night?" he suggested.

"It was eleven o'clock."

"Where the streets would be deserted?"

"Down by Brooklyn Bridge."

"So you met this Mr. Brown and made a deal to touch off your premises."

"That's what I did. Two deals. One was for a flat sum to destroy the papers in my safe. The other was for 25 per cent of the insurance I collected."

"But," Craig objected, "you could have collected your insurance and then refused to divvy up."

"No," the broken man said tearfully. "I got to sign a paper that said what I had hired them to do."

"Didn't you realize," Craig asked, appalled at the man's stupidity, "that they could use that paper to blackmail you all your life?"

"Mister Marshal, I was up against it. I was in a jam. I was desperate. I didn't do no thinking."

"Too bad, friend. But I guess you'll have to come along."

"Where to?"

"First to the Chief Marshal's office. Then the police will take over."

Here, then, was definite proof of commercial arson, with grave possibilities of a lucrative sideline in blackmail. It was organized. It was adroit. Contact between victim and arsonist was made so skillfully that there was no discoverable connecting link. A meeting on a lonely corner in the darkness of the night would make identification of the go-between difficult, even if he and the victim were by some miracle brought face to face. A skillful lawyer could confuse the witness and impeach his identification. And the courts, apt to bend toward the defendant, would make conviction difficult or impossible.

Here, indeed, was a situation such as the Chief Marshal had outlined where direct, definite, irrefutable evidence of an overt act would be difficult to find. The lot of a fire marshal was not an easy one.

Using the power of a fire marshal, which gives him the police authority to arrest—or even to subpoena—Craig led his prisoner to headquarters, and, the matter being of sufficient immediate importance, the Chief Marshal was summoned from his bed. He arrived in no pleasant mood. But for all that, his interrogation was keen, shrewd and searching. The statement of the prisoner was typed and signed by him before he was turned over to the police. It was nearly morning.

The Chief Marshal faced Craig across his flat-topped desk. His eyes were red from lack of sleep and there were tired lines upon his face. He peered at Craig and his gray eyes were narrowed and unfriendly.

"Did I guess the nuisance you were to be," he said bitingly, "you would still be wearing the uniform."

Craig stood mute.

"First," accused the Chief, "ye fetch to me word of a nationwide ring of arsonists and crooks. Then you identify a murdered body as belonging to a member of the Four Hundred. And then you drag in evidence that commercial arson goes on on a big scale in spite of my braggin' that it is wiped out. From you I've had nothing but trouble."

"Yes, sir," Craig answered with a straight face. "Sorry to make trouble, sir."

"Do you dare be fresh with me, young man?" demanded the Chief.

"I would not be so bold," Craig said gravely.

"Go home then to bed." He shook his head ruefully. "I fear you're one of them that trouble follows like a spotted dog once followed a fire engine. I've heard ye called a Typhoid Mary. Bad cess to you for a bloody nuisance."

"Good night, sir," Craig said politely. "I'll try to do better in future."

The Chief stared at the door even after Craig had closed it behind him, and he expelled a deep breath and scowled at his aide. "It looks," he said grimly, "as if business is picking up."

When Craig mounted the stairs to his small apartment he found waiting for him in the hallway an individual of a genus never before encountered in that neighborhood. This person had stepped directly from a comic drawing of the correctest of English man-servants. He wore a dark coat, striped breeches and a bowler hat. On his left hand was a suède glove. His right hand carried its mate. His face was long and lean and closely shaven and his features were of an incredible solemnity. It was not creditable that this apparition could have business with Craig, so the young man stepped past him and inserted his key in the door.

In a high, artificial voice the caricature spoke. "Am I addressing Assistant Fire Marshal Batts?" he inquired.

"That's my name and that's my station," Craig answered. "What can I do for you?"

"I would be honored, sir, if you would permit me to converse with you on a subject which may be of importance to both of us."

Craig pushed open the door and motioned the man to enter. He turned on lights and indicated a comfortable chair.

"It would not be correct for me to sit, sir. Most unsuitable indeed. Am I correctly informed that you are the gentleman who discovered the identity of my late employer, Mr. William Tecumseh Peabody?"

"Right," answered Craig.

"If I may say so, sir, it was a more than ordinarily astute bit of reasoning."

"Thanks," Craig said, "but let's come to the point. Before you wilt."

"I would like, sir, to be assured that I will not be brought into contact with the police—unless, of course, it becomes absolutely necessary. In which event I shall be willing to lay aside my natural prejudice and co-operate to the fullest extent."

"If," Craig replied, "you have pertinent evidence the police will have to know."

The solemn man hesitated; his preternaturally sedate face grew longer. But he straightened his shoulders under his meticulously tailored coat, cleared his throat and said, "My obligation to my late employer compels me to proceed regardless."

"But why this prejudice against the police? I'm a sort of policeman myself."

"My experiences with the metropolitan police, especially with its detective department, have been, to describe them conservatively, unsatisfactory. Until, of course, through the intervention of my late employer I altered my professional status."

"Which was?" asked Craig with interest.

"I may say without undue vanity that I was an exceptionally successful confidence man." He preened himself. "My *modus operandi* was the impersonation of the valet of an English nobleman."

"Do tell!" Craig exclaimed. "And how came you to change your business?"

"I was paroled into the custody of my lamented employer and benefactor. . . . He chanced to be present at my trial, and so impressed was he by my bearing and deportment that he brought influence to bear and took me into his employ. He was so good as to declare that my impersonation was so superb that he never could hope to find a servant to equal me. . . . I may say that during the term of my employment I served him to the best of my not inconsiderable ability."

"An American citizen?"

The man's voice and demeanor altered. He was offended. "Do ye take me for a blasted Britisher? I'll have ye know I was born in Hoboken." He paused and inflated his chest. "My old man was a top-hand peterman, and the old lady was the slickest shoplifter of her time. Me, being puny as a boy, was raised in my former profession."

"I think that entitles you to sit down in my presence," Craig said. "Now what did you come to tell me?"

"My name," he said, "is Japes. When I plied my old trade I was known as Soapy Japes. I wish, sir, that you would accompany me to Mr. Peabody's residence. I have been left in charge by his executors as caretaker. There are things to which your attention should be directed."

"What sort of things, Soapy?"

"Depredations," he replied.

"Is the telephone in operation there?"

"It is." He gave the number.

Craig lifted his own transmitter and spoke to headquarters. "Batts speaking," he said. "I am leaving at once to go to William Tecumseh Peabody's house. You have the address." He gave the telephone number.

"The subway will be quickest," he said, and they went down to the street, neither speaking until they descended to the underground railway and were on their way to Manhattan. They walked to the Peabody residence, which was an imposing edifice of cut stone with mansard roof. Soapy produced a key to the service entrance, and, turning the light switch, led the way to the main floor. It was a large house of many rooms such as had been deemed essential to the wealth and social position of an earlier generation. The furniture was heavy and dark; the wall hangings might have graced a museum. It was, Craig thought as he walked up the gracious curved stairway to the next floor, a meticulously preserved mausoleum. A relic of an era of staidness and conservatism when Mrs. Astor's Four Hundred had been society's all-powerful oligarchy.

"Mr. Peabody's library," Soapy said, as they entered a splendid room whose walls were concealed by bookshelves ceiling high. He pointed. The contents of a bookshelf under an ancestral portrait had been removed and scattered on the Aubusson rug. The portrait above it was wildly askew. A wall safe had been concealed there but its door gaped open.

"Only for intimate and personal papers," Soapy said. "Family records, of course, were in safety deposit."

"Could you state what is missing?" Craig asked.

"For some time before he—ah—absented himself," said Soapy, "he seemed distrait. He shut himself in this room alone writing. He seemed, if I may be so bold, to be depressed. Sad. Sometimes, sir, he spoke to me almost as if I were his equal. In a philosophical manner, if I may put it so. On an occasion, perhaps the last time we spoke before he"—again there was that curious pause and the use of the same circumlocution—"absented himself he looked up at me from his writing, and his expression can be described only as stricken. 'Japes,' he said, 'nations deteriorate. Races become decadent. Old and honorable families forget their traditions, and *noblesse oblige* becomes only an absurd phrase without meaning. These sad descents into Avernus must be expected and endured.' To which I replied 'Yes, sir.' And he went on, blinking his eyes, 'One expects them to occur at a distance, but not in one's immediate circle. It is, Japes, an almost unbearable shock when research, reason and logic place a dear friend in a position so anomalous as to give rise to suspicions that he has become lost to honesty and decency—that, whilst retaining his mental vigor, he has deliberately betrayed his heritage and placed himself without the pale of gentlemen, and become, Japes, a menace to society.' "

"Did you know whom he meant?" Craig asked.

"Nor did I dare ask," Soapy replied. "Mr. Peabody smote his desk with his fist and cried in a voice which I can only describe as agonized, 'Where then does an honorable man's duty lie?' "

Craig sat down in Mr. Peabody's chair, which brought a pained expression to Soapy's face. "So," Craig said half to himself, "Mr. Peabody had discovered or thought he had discovered that a close friend was up to capers. And hadn't made up his mind what to do about it."

"I fancy, sir, he was not given opportunity to make up his mind or to act upon his decision. Without a word to me or the other servants he suddenly was not here. And then he was dead in that undecorous manner."

"Killed," said Craig, "on his way to talk to Chief Fogarty. Why Chief Fogarty, Soapy? Why not the police?"

"I fancy for two reasons," Soapy said. "The first was because the thing that troubled Mr. Peabody had to do with fires—with arson, if I may use that word. The second was because of ancient acquaintance with Chief Patrick Fogarty."

Soapy went to a space on the wall and lifted down a picture incongruous among family portraits and old masters. It was a faded framed photograph, and as Craig examined it he saw that it was of a baseball team. And below each member his name was written, together with the position played. The first name to catch his eye was that written under the picture of a heavily set youth with catcher's mitt in hand. The name was Patrick Fogarty. The pitcher was William Tecumseh Peabody. An outfielder was Harrison Briggs, now president of one of the city's great banks. The third baseman was a politician now high in the councils of Tammany Hall. The second baseman was Pieter Van Rensselaer. The other names made no impression upon Craig Batts. That old boys' team was a strange collection of young aristocrats and youthful members of a lower stratum of society. Perhaps, Craig thought to himself, there had existed more democracy in the age of the glory of Newport than he had supposed.

Underneath the picture, printed in boyish hand, was the legend: *The Old Brewery Nine.*

Here was history. But there was a thing that puzzled Craig Batts. If Chief Fogarty and William Tecumseh Peabody had been teammates forty-odd years ago, why had not the Chief recognized his old playmate on the slab in the morgue?

CHAPTER FIFTEEN

"WHEN," asked Craig, "did you discover that this wall safe had been opened?"

"This afternoon."

"Why did you not report it at once?"

"I am not an impulsive man," Soapy answered. "I reflected. I looked at the matter from all sides. Having reached a decision, I acted."

"Is it your impression," Craig asked, "that Mr. Peabody went to Chief Fogarty rather than to the police because of this very old association?"

"It would be like him. He put great store upon things of the past."

"Can you tell me, Soapy, if he had kept up his friendship with the members of this boys' baseball team?"

"I would doubt it, sir. Perhaps with Mr. Briggs. He was a member of the same club as Mr. Van Rensselaer. Doubtless he would have followed with interest the careers of the others. But he was a gentleman who kept to himself, if you understand that phrase."

"I think I do," Craig said smilingly. "Would you by any chance know where this old brewery was that gave the name to the ball club?"

"Oh, yes, sir. It still stands, though it has long passed into desuetude."

"Into what?"

"It stands idle, sir. And has these many years. As a matter of fact, the land and the building are a part of the Peabody estate.

They were a conservative family of the old style, sir. They never sold. By that I mean that, once they came into possession of a plot of New York real estate, it was almost a religion with them never to part with it. They favored, if I may make the comment, the unearned increment."

"Or, on the contrary, the loss due to the decay of a neighborhood. I should say this brewery property had decreased in value."

"Unquestionably. But Mr. Peabody was confident its value would revive. With the present trend toward the erection of large apartment buildings near the river."

"You say, Soapy, that Mr. Peabody absented himself. By that you mean that he disappeared?"

Soapy nodded in a dignified manner. "He went out before dinner four days before his demise. Leaving no word of his plans."

"He was found, as you probably have read, dressed in a suit of hand-me-down clothes."

Soapy preened himself. "That," he said, "was a confidential matter between my late employer and myself. It was a facet of his personality to possess a sort of romanticism. A thing not altogether unbecoming in a gentleman. He delighted to go abroad on occasions incognito. A thing not without eminent precedent. I believe even a great head of state named Haroun-al-Raschid was wont to seek adventure in this manner."

"You mean, Mr. Peabody would tog himself out in cheap clothes and go out on the town?"

"He did indeed. Sociological research, he called it. It was his intention to write a book. But I prefer to think, sir, that it was a juvenile and romantic search for adventure rather than a serious intention to demean himself by writing a book."

"A bit touched, was he?"

"No more, sir, than is proper in the surviving member of an old and aristocratic line whose—ah—overbreeding may have resulted in mild eccentricity. As to his mind, however, make no mistake, it was acute. It was, if I may venture the comment, sharp as a steel trap."

"And he kept in the house a wardrobe of cheap clothes for use on such forays?"

"Yes, sir."

"Where, Soapy, did he keep them?"

"In a locked closet off his bedroom."

"Suppose we take a look."

"I was meaning to request you to do so. In fact, sir, to make that investigation was the chief reason for my request to come to this house."

"By the way, Soapy, was Mr. Peabody short of funds? Was he in need of money?"

"Indeed not," said Soapy in a shocked voice. "The family investments were such as to be impervious to economic fluctuations."

"Nice for him," Craig commented. And then, "Is this wall safe the only evidence of illegal entry?"

"The only evidence I have detected," said Soapy. "Though they may have prowled the house."

"It seems evident," Craig said, "that the thieves knew what they wanted and where it was to be found. They got it and flitted, not even bothering to close the safe behind them. If they had done that, no one would have known there had been an entry."

"What they did not find and abstract," Soapy said, "will be, perhaps, more significant than what they did find and carry away. If, indeed, they found anything. Mr. Peabody was er—ah—a cagey gentleman. He may have entrusted nothing to this little safe. His diary, or notes, or whatever, might have been entrusted to a less obvious hiding place. But that, sir, is mere speculation. What I have to show you is incontrovertible fact. Will you be so good as to follow me?"

Soapy led the way to the next floor and to the suite of rooms which had been occupied by William Tecumseh Peabody. The bedroom was a large, high-ceilinged room with bay windows across the front. As was the downstairs of the house, this room was heavily furnished in the most expensive ill taste of the Victorian era. At its right was an oblong sitting room, comfortable in spite of its weighty elegance. Soapy walked across this room to open a closet door and stood aside for Craig Batts to enter. Numerous suits dangled from hangers; many pairs of shoes were on a sort of rack. Craig examined the contents of the closet and found nothing to excite his interest.

"Open the little door," Soapy said, and Craig, pushing aside the tailored suits, saw a small door of matched boards which was no more than four feet in height and two and a half feet wide. It was such a door as sometimes gave into low attic rooms under the eaves. Craig opened it and crouched to enter. "You'll need this flashlight, sir," Soapy said, thrusting one through the opening. It was, indeed, a narrow attic space under the slope of the mansard roof. But it was not a hodgepodge of disused rubbish such as one finds in most garrets. It was meticulously neat and organized. Shabby suits hung on hooks, and shabby hats. There was one shoe with a sole four inches thick, such as is worn by one afflicted with clubfoot. Everything seemed to have a place and to occupy it. But what caught Craig's eye immediately were four firemen's uniforms, and four helmets, one with the white panel of a chief!

Craig played the ray of his flash upon these suits of blue. On the hem of one pair of trousers was a daub of red as if it had come into contact with red paint. At the right of these, on a narrow shelf, was a cardboard box which Craig opened. In it were pieces of what seemed to be limp and thin rubber. But upon lifting one of these out it was at once apparent that they were the sort of rubber masks which are pulled over the head.

These were the things which had given the men who emerged from the jewelry store with their loot that strange, inhuman, robot-like appearance that Craig had noted before he had taken the blow that had rendered him unconscious.

In his mind was no doubt that here, before his eyes, were those identical rented uniforms worn by the looters. The immediate question then was: How had they come into possession of William Tecumseh Peabody? Was this eminent, conservative aristocrat a part of a criminal organization that preyed from coast to coast? Had some quirk of inbreeding caused him to be traitor to all traditions of family and class and send him seeking adventure in the criminal world?

Such a thing was possible. Craig had read enough of abnormal psychology to know that even stranger things than this happened to the aberrant human mind. A double personality, a split ego. Or, perhaps and more regrettably, the deliberate choice of a life of crime!

Craig backed out of the narrow space, leaving the disguises where he had found them. Soapy awaited him, standing with almost comical dignity and expressionlessness of face.

"Well," Craig asked, "so what?"

"So," said Soapy, relaxing for the instant his pose of the perfect servant, "so what-what?"

"You know what these things are?"

"I called for you to show them to you," Soapy said.

"You draw some conclusion?"

"One would, naturally, sir."

"And that conclusion is?"

"That on one of his expeditions my late employer found these garments and masks, and brought them here, he being well aware of their significance."

"Would you say that possession of these uniforms indicated guilt?"

"Definitely not, sir," Soapy said emphatically. "I would aver that they indicate innocence. That they indicate a certain enterprise on the part of my late employer which led him to this discovery and moved him to impound this evidence. Far from indicating guilt, sir, I would insist that they led to his death at the hands of those who are guilty."

"Then why," Craig demanded, "did he not hand this evidence over to the police?"

"Who can say, sir, what motives rule such a man as Mr. Peabody? This I will say without fear of contradiction, that he was on the side of the law. That some lack of final and conclusive proof compelled him to retain possession. In the thinking of such a man with such antecedents *noblesse oblige* might be a ruling force. If he had to choose between *noblesse oblige* and the obligation of a good citizen, there might ensue a heartbreaking struggle."

Craig half closed his eyes and concentrated upon a thought. He never had entertained a thought of that nature before. Was *noblesse oblige* an exclusive possession of the highly born, of the elite? Or was it thinkable that it might be a compelling thing in the life of one more humbly born—say, of a fireman? He stood motionless, grappling with the problem, with a personal conundrum. Could that phrase of chivalry account for the strange behavior of his Uncle Paddy, of Nora's father, of Chief Patrick Fogarty? Were that grand old Mick, Paddy Fogarty, and that aristocrat of aristocrats, William Tecumseh Peabody, brothers in chivalry under their skins? Why not? There had been kings in Ireland. Might not Uncle Paddy have derived from one of them?

114

Of one thing Craig was certain. Whether or not the laws of chivalry and panoplied knights and horrid dragons and Merlin the magician himself were concerned in this bewildering, kaleidoscopic mystery, he would stand guard over this evidence, nor would he desert it for one instant until it should be delivered into the custody of the Chief Fire Marshal of the City of New York.

"Soapy," he said, "go to the telephone and call this number. It is the Fire Marshal's office. Say that you are calling for Assistant Fire Marshal Craig Batts. Tell whoever answers to burn the wires and the pavements, but to get the Chief here faster than he ever went anywhere before. Say to him that hell has busted loose in the vineyard and he'd better get here with an extinguisher."

"Then," said Soapy lugubriously, "I'll be dragged into it?"

"And maybe," said Craig impatiently, "have a medal planted on your pigeon breast."

"Very good, sir. I understand and condone the necessity."

Craig stood before the closet door as if afraid to move a step from that position. Soapy walked to the telephone, dialed the number Craig had given him and then, realizing he had heard no dial tone, replaced the instrument on its cradle and tried again. He called to Craig in a startled voice, "No dial tone, sir. The line is dead."

"Hang up and try again."

Soapy obeyed with the same result. "Either, sir," he said formally, "the telephone is out of order or it has been tampered with."

"When did you use it last?"

"Not for a considerable time, sir."

Craig considered the situation. It was possible that the phone had gone out of business through mechanical failure, as telephones sometimes do. But that would be too fortuitous. It was more likely that the line had been tampered with. But why? What reason had anyone to put this particular telephone out of business? Unless it had been an instinctive measure of precaution when Mr. Peabody's apartment had been ransacked. But that did not seem logical. It was more reasonable to deduce that Soapy Japes had been observed to bring Craig to the house by watchers. That Craig had been recognized as a fire marshal and that the telephone had been silenced to prevent his calling headquarters. That could indicate only that the criminals had not found all they were searching for when they had entered and opened Mr. Peabody's wall safe; that they had been interrupted and put to flight, and were waiting a safer opportunity to continue their search of the premises.

In which case it must be true that they were either in the house itself or were in a spot from which they could observe and from which they could act promptly in case of necessity.

So, Craig said to himself, they saw me come in. Brought by Soapy. Not being half-witted, they reasoned that Soapy had brought me for a purpose, which could only be to show me something. And that something would be the thing for which they themselves had searched. The uniforms and the rubber masks!

But then came another and disturbing thought. If Mr. William Tecumseh Peabody were guiltily concerned in the robbery of the jewelry store and were the custodian for the gang for this evidence, why should his home be searched as it had been? Why should the house be watched, if he were? Why should the telephone wire have been cut, if, indeed, it had? . . . And, to go much, much farther, why had Mr. Peabody been abducted, as seemed to be the fact, and held a prisoner—and murdered?

Here surely was a puzzle. Or were there wheels within wheels? Some sort of internecine warfare among members of the criminal organization itself?

Craig, while he reasoned about the situation, was making a bundle of the uniforms and other bits of evidence. There was no string or rope with which to make it fast, so he searched for some makeshift and found a collection of four-in-hand neckties in a dresser drawer. With these he proceeded to make the garments into a sort of bale while Soapy stood by, uttering from time to time a gasp of dismay.

"Why the puffing and panting?" Craig asked.

"Sir," Soapy exclaimed with horror as if Craig had been desecrating some shrine, "do you realize what you are doing? That you are using a number of Countess Mara ties as if they were so much string!"

"Mr. Peabody won't be using them," Craig said.

"But—works of art, sir!"

Craig pushed the drawer to close it, but it would not shut. Something was clogging it. He pushed harder, but the drawer still remained a couple of inches open. He pulled it out and set it on the floor and then reached back into the resulting opening. Something was there. He brought it out where he could see it. It was a manila envelope and fragments of scotch tape clung to it. Craig eyed it with puckered brows. Then he knelt and scrutinized the orifice from which he had removed the drawer. What had happened was evident. The envelope had been fastened to the underside of the top of the dresser with adhesive tape. There had been sufficient space for the drawer to work back and forth. But it had become loosened by Craig and dropped from its place of concealment.

He held it up for Soapy to see. "What's this?" he asked.

"I never saw it before, sir. I was not aware of its presence in that place."

Craig tucked it under his arm and picked up his clumsy bale of uniforms. "We'd better scram out of here while the scramming is good," he said. "If we can."

At the top of the stair well Craig listened. The house was silent. Behind him Soapy pressed a switch and stairway and hall were immediately brightly lighted. With caution they descended. Still there was no sound, no sign of intruders in the old family mansion. They reached the main floor. Before them were the vestibule and the great, carved front doors. Nothing, so far, had interfered with their departure. But Craig was not happy; in his subconscious a tocsin sounded.

"There's nobody in this house," he said positively. "You can *feel* there's nobody here. . . ." He stood still as a statue and listened. Only sounds of evening traffic on the street outside were audible.

"Where's the basement door?" he asked peremptorily. It was as if he did not ask the question of his own volition but because of some instinctive prompting.

"Here, sir," Soapy directed. He led the way and opened a door into the dark cavern below. His fingers found the light switch and the basement leaped into view. Craig descended the stairs with Soapy at his heels. At the bottom he stood motionless again, listening. A faint ticking came to his ears, as of a muffled clock. It seemed to come from beneath his feet, but as he moved cautiously he located the sound behind a partition of matched boarding beneath the wooden stairs. He tore open the door and the ticking was louder.

It was a strangely cluttered closet. Not neat as was the rest of

117

the basement which was visible. It was crammed with excelsior, and the excelsior smelled peculiarly and was damp to the touch.

Craig scrambled in the mass. His fingers contacted a square container, and recklessly he snatched it from its place of concealment. The box of light wood was a foot or more square, and from its interior the ticking continued. Craig snatched open the hinged top and tore from its fastening the wire that ran from the clock to a container. No explosion followed. No burst of sound and flame. He stood shaking, suddenly aware of his folly, that this was no way in which to deal with an infernal machine. But, more by good luck than good judgment, he had rendered it harmless. He stood staring down at the intricate mechanism. It was no clumsy makeshift thing, but a device constructed with skill and efficiency. He was aware of an odor and sniffed the air.

"What's the stink?" he asked shakily.

"Why, sir, I believe that to be the characteristic odor of an explosive named nitrocellulose. My father—"

"Right," Craig snapped. "Can you carry it?"

"I can manage it, sir."

They climbed the stairs and went out the front door to the street, where they stood on the walk signaling for a taxicab. Presently one swung into the curb and they scrambled inside with their impedimenta. Craig gave the address of headquarters. They settled back upon the seat, and Craig heaved a sigh.

"Soapy," he said, "I guess we can tie a knot in our neckscarf. We've done our good deed for the day."

CHAPTER SIXTEEN

THE CHIEF MARSHAL sat behind his desk. In a chair at his left was Lieutenant Fisano of the police department. Soapy Japes and Craig Batts occupied chairs against the side wall of the office. On a table were spread four uniforms and rubber masks which Craig had brought to headquarters. Chief Marshal was opening the manila envelope which Craig had found behind the drawer in William Tecumseh Peabody's dresser. It contained papers of different sizes. They had been clipped from books or periodicals. The first which the Chief picked up was a chapter from a treatise on abnormal psychology. The second was an article in more popular language taken from a magazine and entitled "Pyromania." There were two other pieces dealing with mental aberrations, and a letter from the head of a mental institution which said:

Dear William:

There is nothing in the data you send me to indicate that the individual about whom you inquire is off his trolley. Of course a definite opinion could not be given without examination of the individual himself. It is possible, by stating isolated facts about the behavior of any individual, to establish a *prima facie* case of unsound mind.

However, I may say that it is wholly within the bounds of possibility for any human being to possess a brilliant mind and at the same time criminal tendencies. I am not even prepared to aver that the commission of a crime or of a series of crimes is abnormal in the sense that it indicates a diseased mind. One must know all the facts. A sane man, through pressures, may deliberately choose a criminal career. Who can state positively that a moral, upright life is not artificial, produced by moral teachings and/or a fear of consequences? No, William, you have made out a case for eccentricity but not for mental illness. My conclusion from your data is that the man is simply a bad egg.

"Now what," asked Fisano, "do you make of that?"

The Chief looked at Craig. "Deduce," he said, half ironically.

"That is easy," Craig answered. "Mr. Peabody had an acquaintance, maybe a friend, and he knew or suspected that he was leading a double life. On the surface a good citizen, but actually a criminal. And he was trying by reading and by consultation with a specialist to find out if this man was nuts. It wouldn't be farfetched to conclude that he wanted to find out if this person were a pyromaniac or a sane arsonist."

"I agree," Fisano said. "But there's no clue to the identity of the man."

"None that I can see," Craig replied.

"Could all this," the Chief asked, "be worry about himself? I mean is it possible that Peabody was afraid for his own sanity? That maybe he drew mental blanks and was afraid of what he did in those periods?"

"I'd say it was definitely possible," Fisano said. "Even probable. You know he may even have found these uniforms and masks in his own possession and couldn't remember how he got them." He turned to Soapy Japes. "You saw more of your employer than anybody else did. Would you say he was crackers?"

"My considered judgment, sir, is that Mr. Peabody was sane. Somewhat peculiar, perhaps, but nevertheless of a high order of intelligence."

"But these night wanderings in more or less disguise?" Fisano suggested.

"I can only assert, sir, that my late employer, in my opinion, had excellent reason for what he did. Sometimes, gentlemen, he did things which, at the moment, seemed peculiar. But in many instances, to my personal knowledge, they turned out to have been done with reason and foresight. He—er—to quote from Holy Writ, moved often in a mysterious way his wonders to perform."

The Chief, for the moment, abandoned the baffling personality of William Tecumseh Peabody and lifted from the floor the light plywood box containing the infernal machine. "A new wrinkle in gadgets," he said. "Not much that wouldn't be destroyed when the nitrocellulose went off. That's about as hotly inflammable stuff as there is."

"I doubt," Craig said thoughtfully, "if the idea was to conceal the cause of the fire, but was to make sure there was a hot one that went off at a determined time. With this clockwork thing it could be set to go at any time within twenty-four hours. It's an expensive little clock and would keep good time."

Lieutenant Fisano drummed on the desk top with slender but powerful fingers. "We've got to start thinking somewhere," he said, "and the most obvious taking-off place is these uniforms. . . . First question: did Peabody have custody of them for the gang? Or did he find them somewhere and lug them away for evidence? On one of these queer snooping expeditions of his did he happen on where they were stashed and lug them home? For the sake of argument, let's make an assumption and see where it leads us."

"What assumption?" asked the Chief Marshal.

"That Peabody was an honest man and on the side of the law. Soapy, with the best opportunity to observe him, says that is the case. All right, he had a yen to play cops and robbers. But, accepting my assumption, he must have been making a systematic investigation based upon suspicion. He must have seen or heard something that set him to sniffing. There must have been some clue he discovered and was following up. And there must have been some person or persons that he suspected."

"That red chief's car the four robbers rode in," said Craig. "It vanished as if it had disintegrated. It was driven off the street into some place of concealment, where it could be repainted."

"Leading up to what?" asked the Chief.

"To the conclusion that Mr. Peabody must have found that place. The uniforms and masks indicate that. Somehow, without being seen, he must have gained admission to that place and made off with the evidence."

"Reasonable, if our assumption of his innocence is correct. But

121

if he was on the level, why didn't he turn the stuff over to the police?"

"We can only guess that for some reason he wanted to make a complete case by himself," Craig said. "Now a next reasonable assumption is that he went back to that hiding place and was nabbed by the gang. He escaped and was going with what he knew to Chief Fogarty when he was shot."

"Why didn't they bump him off in the first place?" Fisano wanted to know.

"Probably he was caught by some subordinates who didn't want to act without orders from above," Craig said.

"So they searched his house and robbed his wall safe—but didn't make a thorough rummage. Or they would have found the uniforms in that closet," Craig said.

"And," said the Chief, "set the infernal machine to conceal the fact that they had broken in."

"Or," said Craig, "to destroy the evidence they had not found."

Lieutenant Fisano got to his feet. He was not exactly a handsome man, but, Craig thought, he would be attractive to women. His eyebrows were Mephistophelean but the eyes were a liquid brown. His mouth was not girlish, though many a girl would have liked to have it. He was slender but weighed more than he appeared to weigh, and he would be a tough customer in a fracas.

"We'll get no farther this night. Only addle our brains batting this thing back and forth," he said. "I'm for bed."

They all left the office and descended to the street. It was close to midnight. All but Soapy and Craig traveled northward. Soapy seemed hesitant. Craig guessed the reason.

"You're not exactly eager to sleep in the Peabody house tonight," he said. "Don't blame you. I've got a davenport in my living room. It'll be comfortable and you're welcome."

"I would appreciate it, sir," he said, "but I must not accept. I have been retained as custodian of the residence, and a custodian must not absent himself."

"Good night, then," Craig said. "Keep in touch."

"I will do so, sir," Soapy said deferentially. And then, "It is gratifying to be entrusted with responsibility." He smiled crookedly. "I doubt if the lawyers would have been so complaisant had they been aware of my antecedents."

122

Craig walked to the subway and rode to Brooklyn. He mounted the stairs to his small apartment. Speedily he undressed and went to bed, but weary as he was sleep did not come to him at once. He lay with eyes open staring at the dimness of the room and strove to fit together the pieces of the jigsaw puzzle that lay in a jumble before him. But the pieces would not dovetail. He shut his eyes and closed his mind. He was able to clear it and to concentrate on nothingness. Presently he slept. He did not awake by degrees in the morning, nor bask in semisomnolence. When he opened his eyes he was wide awake. It always had been so with him—one instant sound asleep, the next instant awake and alert.

In his tiny kitchenette he brewed coffee, fried eggs and bacon and browned toast. After breakfast he cleaned up after himself with exactitude and made his way to headquarters. Once in the office he sat at his desk and put in writing his report of the previous day's activities. Before he had set all down on paper it was close to noon. There remained in the office but three or four of his fellow marshals, among whom was his mentor, Luke Priddy, who came to stand beside his desk.

"Graduated from my class, seems as though," Priddy said with his grin which was a humorous mixture of irony and friendship. "Scuttlebutt says you had a day yesterday."

"Just stumbled into things," Craig said deprecatingly.

"Better good luck than good judgment," Priddy said. "Me, I'd rather have luck than brains. I just got brains. How about we go to lunch?" He flexed his shoulders and let his eyes travel around the room. "Haven't stumbled onto who swiped that file out of the cabinet, have you?"

"I wonder why it's important," Craig said. "Where'll we eat?"

"How about Luigi's?" Priddy asked.

They walked a couple of blocks to the large and busy Italian restaurant and were able to find seats in a stall on the right side of the room which contained a table for four with a bench on either side. They crowded in and gave their orders. The waiter had moved away but a couple of steps when a gentleman stopped at the end of the table and asked in a cultivated voice, "Young gentlemen, may I join you for luncheon?"

"Why, surely, Mr. Van Rensselaer," Craig said, moving over. "Do you know Assistant Marshal Priddy?"

"I've not had that pleasure," the dapper gentleman said, affixing his monocle in his eye and scrutinizing Craig's companion.

"But I," Priddy said, "recognize the king of the buffs."

Mr. Van Rensselaer simpered. "A title I may covet but scarcely merit," he said. "Your profession is my avocation," he added. " have not encountered you, Mr. Batts, since the day of the robbery of the jewelry store, when you were so unfortunately assaulted." He let his monocle drop and dangle. "I recall you now, Mr. Priddy You were present that day."

Craig, to be polite, continued the conversation. "Long befor you became a buff," he said, "I'm told you were quite a baseba player."

"Why, yes—yes." He returned his monocle to his eye and peere at Craig a bit frostily. "Now I wonder how you came by such piece of information."

Caution closed Craig's mouth. That old team photograph wa evidence and the property of the Bureau of Fire Investigation. H evaded the question. "It might have been Uncle Paddy," he said "He was on the team, wasn't he?"

"He was, indeed," answered Van Rensselaer. "I hope Chie Fogarty has made a complete recovery."

"He is his old self again."

"Physically," said Van Rensselaer. His over-refined face set i harsh lines. It astonished Craig that his expression was one o malignancy rather than of anger. "Rely upon it, young man," h said, "the man who caused that injury will pay for it a dozen times I, myself, will see to it."

"That," Craig said gravely, "is not a matter for a private citizen."

"It is a matter for this private citizen," Van Rensselaer retorted There was venom in his voice, a poison that was wholly out o character and which did not fit in either with the event or wit the man's bearing or reputation. It seemed to Craig to be a persona thing, as a feud may be a personal thing to a Kentucky moun taineer. Surely Van Rensselaer did not love Uncle Paddy so fondl as to cause him to exhibit such malice against his assailant. Ther was more behind it than was apparent to the eye, and Craig curiosity was excited by it. A thought entered his mind and re fused to be ejected—that the little, dapper, monocled man knew th perpetrator and hated him for reasons of his own, which, manifestly, was impossible.

Then occurred a coincidence—or was it a coincidence? Craig's mind rejected the fortuitous until the possibility of intention or plan could be definitely eliminated. Coincidences did occur, and surprisingly, but they offended Craig's sense of order and logic. A fourth man paused at the table and spoke in a strangely, intentionally irritating voice.

"I hope," said Clyde Tupper, "that you gentlemen will not object to my occupying the vacant seat. There seems to be no other in the restaurant."

"You," Craig said in a chill voice, "are welcome as a skunk at a strawberry festival."

"Always gracious," Tupper said, and seated himself in the vacant place across the table from Van Rensselaer.

Craig's eyes were drawn to the slender man's face. It was purple, apoplectic. Literally he was choking with rage. He struggled for self-control and achieved it.

"The concession hawker!" he said sneeringly.

"Does that render me *déclassé?*" Tupper asked in a voice so mild that it was provocative. He turned to the other two. "If you want a spot for a vending machine in the subway, you come to me. Or the privilege of selling hot dogs and coffee at a county fair. Or peanuts at a street carnival."

"Or protection for slot machines," said Van Rensselaer, "or maybe a drop in the numbers racket."

"Beware of actionable slander," said Tupper amiably. "Temper! Temper! Unworthy of a member of one of our first families."

"Did you follow me here?" Van Rensselaer demanded.

"Why should I? Of what interest to me are your places to lunch?"

Craig tipped his head to one side and smiled a twisted smile at Tupper. "He may not, Mr. Van Rensselaer, be so infatuated with you that he trails you about town, but, as for himself, there seems to be someone on *his* tail. Maybe it's a personification of conscience, Tupper."

"Meaning what, Batts?"

Craig pointed. Outside the door of the restaurant, staring in through the window, was Annie Mertz.

"She said," Craig added, "that she was going to stick to you like a bloodhound. If I were in your place I think I'd worry a little."

"Batts," Tupper said tensely, and there was, indeed, apprehension in his eyes, "you have influence with that damn girl. Move her off my neck, before I have to spray with Flit."

"This," Craig said conversationally to the others at the table, "is a lesson in deportment. It teaches not to tamper with beautiful little sisters."

Tupper slid out of the seat and stood in the aisle.

"Lost your appetite?" Craig asked.

Van Rensselaer was completely himself again, aristocratic, urbane, the polished gentleman.

"A competent physician," he said to no one in particular, "might advise Mr. Tupper to revise his habits lest he lose his appetite permanently."

With no retort Tupper strode away and went out, not through the front door where Annie Mertz stood, but through a side door onto another street.

Craig shrugged and addressed himself to his plate of spaghetti. He managed it skillfully. After a few mouthfuls he spoke to Van Rensselaer without lifting his eyes.

"You seem to be an ill-wisher to Mr. Tupper," he said.

"Quite vigorously so," said the older gentleman.

"Would it," Craig asked at a venture—actually without volition, but because the question popped into his head, "would it be so vigorous as to shoot bullets at him out of a passing car?"

"Now that," Van Rensselaer said mildly, "is what might be termed an indiscreet question."

"So it was," Craig admitted. "So it was. I withdraw it. But could I ask a question about the old brewery baseball team?"

"Suppose you pose your question, and then we will see."

"Right," Craig said. "What has that old baseball nine got to do with the robbery of the jewelry store at which you were present as a buff? And what has it to do with the stranglehold Tupper seems to have on Uncle Paddy Fogarty?"

"You," said Van Rensselaer with twinkling eyes—and to Craig it seemed a genuine twinkle, "have thrown in your hook where there

126

are no fish. . . . And so, young gentlemen, a good afternoon to you both."

He too made his dignified way out of the restaurant and left Craig and Priddy staring at each other in a nonplused manner.

"This proves," Craig said presently, "that you can't tell by looking at a frog which way he will jump."

"Right," agreed Priddy.

Craig finished his coffee and sighed. "There are too darn many inbred and aristocratic gentlemen in this case to suit me."

"Batts," Priddy said thoughtfully, "my considered judgment is that someday, instead of stumbling into something, you're going to stumble over something and bust your beak."

"And that," Craig said heavily, "could bloody well be the truth."

CHAPTER SEVENTEEN

IT WAS a Sunday afternoon and Craig Batts was not on duty. He had walked home from church with Nora Fogarty, an early service, and the whole day lay before them. Nora was lovely in a powder-blue tailored suit and pert hat that did not conceal the crisp yet soft waviness of her hair. Craig was trim and athletic in a gabardine suit with the corner of a handkerchief peeping from the breast pocket of his coat. He needed no padding for his shoulders. Nora, looking at him out of the corner of her Irish eyes, was quite satisfied with his appearance, which she did not mention. She wondered if he were pleased with her trim appearance.

They were halted by the traffic, which gave Craig opportunity to light a cigarette, and as he put away his lighter he inspected her with brotherly eye. But as his glance swept upward from toe to topknot the glance lost something of brotherliness and became definitely interested—so interested, indeed, that he did not notice that traffic had changed and they could cross the street.

"Taking a nap?" Nora asked.

He started and grinned. "No, Gumdrop," he said, "I was just giving you the once-over."

"What brought that up?" she demanded.

"I just happened to notice you," he said.

"You could have done that any day these twenty years," she snapped.

"No percentage in noticing kids," he said. "When did you outgrow it?"

"About the time you stopped having pimples," she said.

He nodded his head. "You're grown up," he said, and then, squinting his eyes, "Seems to me I've noticed it coming on. In spots. But it never impressed me until just now."

"What spots?" she asked pertly.

"How old are you anyhow?"

"Old enough," she said shortly.

"It sort of alters things, doesn't it?" he said thoughtfully.

"Meaning what?"

"Meaning I can't just let you tag along any more." He seemed to have some difficulty expressing himself. "I mean, up to now, it's been sort of impersonal, like we were a couple of kids. Not people but kids. Not even boy and girl but—er—sort of—" He couldn't find the right word.

"Sexless," she supplied.

The word shocked him, but there was no other term for it. He walked along a hundred feet without speaking while he thought that phase of it over.

"Maybe that's it," he said finally.

"Definitely that's it," she said.

"It makes a difference," he said. "I don't know if I like it."

"That," she said, her sprightly head on one side and mischief in her eyes, "that depends."

"Upon what?" he asked.

"Upon how it turns out," she rejoined. "It depends on whether you keep on being a stupid oaf or if you get your eyes open—like a kitten. . . ." She stamped her foot and nearly turned her ankle in the process and said an unladylike word.

"Mind telling me what you're hinting at?"

"Not in the least," she said tartly. "You've been playing around with me for darn near twenty years as if I were a puppy. Or maybe a small boy you're somehow related to. Well, Mr. Batts, I'm sick and tired of it. You've got to make up your stupid mind whether I'm fish, flesh or good red herring. And go on from there. Beginning now you can darn well make up your mind. You've got choices. I've got choices. Let's start with basic facts. I'm a woman and a pretty choice one if I do say it myself. I'm a dish. And if you don't think other men have noticed it, just walk past the next drugstore with me and listen to the whistles."

"All right," he said. "You're a dish. You're a six-power dish. But what of it?"

"This of it," she said. "You can either cut and run and go sell your papers. Or you can yield to natural impulses and make a pass, which would get your face slapped. Or you can lay siege. One of the three, me lad. But you can't just dangle around and take me for granted. Either, Mr. Batts, you make a two-fisted play for me, or you turn in your chips."

"Well," gasped Craig, "I'll be darned."

"You're darned right you'll be darned," she said. "So look me over again and take stock and make up your feeble mind whether you want to plunge into what the last generation called a courtship, or not."

"You mean you want me to light a torch for you?"

"Yes," she said promptly.

"You mean," he asked embarrassedly, "that you like me that way?"

"I didn't say that, and far from it. Maybe I do. Maybe I don't. That's for you to find out. . . . Girls are smarter than boys. A ten-year-old girl has more know-how than a twenty-five-year-old boy. Since I was ten, Mister, I've had a yen for you. I've figured you might grow up into what I want."

"Have I?" he asked.

"All but mentally," she said.

"Look here, Trinket, are you telling me you're in love with me?"

"I'm telling you," she said, "that the walls of Jericho might come tumbling down if you marched around hard enough and blew horns loud enough. But if you think a fruit like me drops off the bough into any man's lap while he just sits, then you're silly. Whoever picks me has got to climb and reach."

"This," he said ruefully, "is the darnedest conversation I ever heard. I bet it's what they call unique."

"Because," she retorted, "I'm unique."

"That you can repeat," he said, and stared at her with eyes that saw a new picture and a desirable picture and a compelling picture. "Doggone," he said in some bewilderment, "such an idea never entered my head before."

"Well, it better enter now—or, as Grandma used to say: Skiddoo!"

"Woman," he said, "don't try to rush me into something. It's a new idea. I've got to let it sink in." He made a malignant face. "If Uncle Paddy heard you talking like this, he'd paddle your little behind."

"You'd be surprised to know that he wouldn't," she said briskly.

"Let's have sixty seconds of silence," he said peremptorily. "Desist from deafening me with your clatter whilst I give thought."

So they walked along in silence. His face was solemn, but there was a mischievous glint in Nora's eyes as she waited. From time to time he looked at her with calculating scrutiny. At the end of not one minute but several, he stopped and faced her and she stopped and faced him.

"Turn your ear, Sugar Plum," he said, and his voice was grave. "If 'twas just arms and legs and a face that is beautiful that I want, I would reach out my arms and grasp ye to me. But I'm studying what I know of ye and your thoughts and your ways, and if there's poetry in you and what they call fortitude and essential guts, so to say, and understandin' and all those qualities that have to be there after ye get out of bed, to hold a marriage strong and permanent. And you, Nora Fogarty, should be askin' the same about me before we take ary step from which there's no drawing back."

"And how," she asked, eyes somber, "do we find the truth of those questions?"

He grinned. It was a broad, merry, Irish grin, and it made her heart flutter. "It was for that purpose that Heaven, aided and abetted by the good saints and by bad nature, ordained that there should be courtships."

"Yes?" she said with rising inflection.

"Consequently," he said, "in the interests of you and me and a contented life and the arriving of future generations, I am about to start, and will continue to wage, the biggest and searchingest and busiest two-fisted courtship ever was heard of since there were kings in Ireland." He paused and waggled his head. "And I may say, Jelly Bean, that I'm at the present moment lookin' forward to it with clutchin' anticipation."

"Very well," she said demurely. "Commence. Give samples."

It was curious, but a shyness overtook both of them as they walked the rest of the distance to the Fogartys' apartment, and it did not leave them as they entered the little parlor where Chief

Fogarty sat reading the morning paper in his stocking feet. He looked up at them casually and then his steel-gray eyes sharpened and he glowered under beetling brows.

"What has come over the two of ye this Sunday morning?" he demanded. "From all brands of foolishness defend us!"

"We would not know how foolish," Craig said. "But this daughter of yours, whose tongue wags at both ends, has just argued me into paying court to her."

"Is it so?" the Chief demanded. "Then begone the both of you into the fields and woods and watery places. For little of the truth of such matters is to be found pent between four walls. The beginning and the end of it should be where great trees throw their shade and soft breezes wave the grass. And wee birds look down and sing a song of gr-reat wisdom. Away wid the both of ye."

He returned to his newspaper and rattled it fiercely, nor would he have another word to say to either of them.

They went down to the street and to the garage where Craig kept his small, second-hand car, and then, in the gay sunshine, drove out the south shore of the island, and it was Nora who set the tone and manner of their conversation. One moment she laughed at everything they saw and at everything he said, and was pert and merry; and the next moment she was serious and wanted to discuss grave matters such as the affairs of nations and books she had read, but never another word of what had been talked between them an hour ago.

Nor did they put into words their worry about Uncle Paddy Fogarty and what secret might lie between him and Clyde Tupper. For both of them wanted this to be a light, careless day with no shadows on it. But, womanlike, Nora could not hold to the impersonal.

"Now," she said, "that you have left the uniformed branch and become a marshal, are you content?"

"For the day and the hour I am content," he told her.

"And what does that mean—the day and the hour?"

"Why, sure enough," he told her, "I want the day to come when I ride in my own red car with an aide to drive me and even rise to be Chief of Department. With all the pay and the honors. But before I set my mind to that there is a thing I must try to do."

"Your father! But his death was long ago. How many years?"

"Six," said Craig.

"And neither police nor fire marshal has been able to get to the truth of it? If, in all that time, no progress could be made, how can you hope to do more at this late day?"

"All those others," Craig said somberly, "did not have it laid upon them as such a matter is laid upon a son."

That she was able to understand, the personal, filial obligation to avenge the death of a parent. Such comprehension was in her blood, come down from Celtic ancestors south of the Derry wall, to whom the blood feud had been a savage, sacred obligation.

"But how will you search, Craig? Where will you look?"

"More secret crimes," he said, "are revealed by the fears of the guilty than by any searching and seeking by the police. If the guilty would be content, and sit tight and make no movement, they would be safe from detection. But they are afraid. They do some silly thing that calls attention to them—in an effort to make themselves safe. And then—"

She nodded. "But after so long what can happen to worry them?"

"I think something has happened. I think they have done that foolish thing. They, or he, made the first move when I was appointed to my new job. The file containing the papers in the case were stolen from among the records."

She was silent, thinking it over. After a time she said softly, "Craig, you mustn't let this thing warp you or twist you."

"That I shall not do," he said firmly.

"But," she said, "I have known men and women who became obsessed, who became possessed by a single thing to the exclusion of everything else. To their ruin."

"It shall not be so with me," he assured her. "I loved my father. I would, indeed, make the guilty one pay, but not to the point of unbalancing my mind or ruining my life." And then he grinned, but there was more than mirth in the grin. There was something grim in the expression. "Besides," he said, "I think there will not be a long time to addle me." He nodded his head. "I've a premonition the end of it all is not far distant. There are many loose pieces, but I think they are parts of a whole. My father's murder. A professional arsonist who advertises. The thing between your father and Tupper. The shooting of William Tecumseh Peabody. Four firemen's uniforms and four rubber masks. An infernal machine in Peabody's basement. I think they are all parts of a single whole, though I've no evidence to back me. Only a feeling."

"Intuition," said Nora.

"And, maybe most important of all," said Craig, once more speaking words not formed in his waking mind but in the subconscious, "a kids' baseball team that played in a brewery yard." He heard what he had said with surprise, with shock. He sat staring at the road and did not hear her when she spoke to him.

"It is after noon," she said.

He did not hear or heed.

"Do you start this whirlwind courtship you bragged about by starving the lady?" she asked more sharply.

He looked at her without comprehension. Then the sense of her words penetrated. "Sure," he said, "I'll ply you with chowder and smoked eels and clam pie. And we will sit with bare feet in the sand. And then we will go home the long way—over Queensborough Bridge and down the East Side Drive. For, all of a sudden, Popsicle, I've a yearning to drive past the door of an ancient and long idle buildin' that once was a brewery for making beer."

CHAPTER EIGHTEEN

THE OLD building of red brick was of the brewery school of architecture of the 1880's; castle-on-the-Rhine motif with towers and turrets and bastions. Craig drove slowly past its face, and it was a dead face with blank eyes. At the left of the front were huge doors through which handsome brewery horses used to prance with wagon high-piled with kegs of beer behind them. That had been so long ago that Craig, born in the mechanical age, had never seen the spectacle. He drove around the block twice, but the structure had no story to tell.

"Well," Nora said, after circling the block three times, "I'm all for a change of scenery. I've got this example of beer architecture committed to memory."

"I'd like to snoop around inside," Craig told her.

"I doubt if you'd be welcome," she said. "The caretaker or somebody has been watching us from a third-story window."

"Your eyes are better than mine," Craig said.

"Because you were studying the ground floor," Nora said. "Do caretakers wear glasses?"

"I doubt if there's a law against it."

"Because the sun glinted from something. That was what attracted my attention." She knit her brows. "I got an impression it was Cyclopean."

"There ought to be a law," he growled, "against women meddling with higher education. It's not tactful. It gives their husbands an inferiority complex."

"When you get one of those," she said crisply, "it'll be the day!"

"So happens," Craig said airily, to put her in her place, "that I'm hep to Cyclops." He frowned suddenly. "Are you sure, Ginger Cookie, it was a single lens?"

"Not to raise my hand and swear," she admitted. "But I got the impression of oneness."

"A caretaker with glasses," Craig said thoughtfully, "I can swallow. But a watchman with a monocle sticks in my craw."

"Maybe it's a result of a share-the-wealth program," she said. "Maybe a street cleaner, in this welfare state, is as much entitled to wear a monocle as a member of the peerage."

"Good political slogan: Monocles for the multitude."

"Or a television program," she said. "For one buck you can buy a monocle and join the aristocracy."

There was no sound of a shot, but a star made its appearance in the windshield. Craig felt the wind of a bullet as it passed within an inch of his temple. It had not been fired from the brewery but from behind the high board fence on the north side of the street. Craig stepped on the accelerator and whisked the car around the corner.

"Silencer," he said grimly.

"I wouldn't like it even if it went *bang!*" Nora said.

"If you weren't here," Craig said morosely.

"But I am," she said, "and I want to go away from here. Before your simply headlong courtship ends with an obituary."

"Aren't you frightened?" he asked, turning to look at her lovely but expressionless profile.

"Why should I be?" she asked. "They weren't gunning for me."

"Brainless!" Craig exclaimed.

"Who? Me?"

"The laddy who shot the bullet," he said. "Calling attention to this neighborhood."

Craig drove over to Park Avenue and turned southward. "Cleared out of there," he said, "because I'd be no good at all to you if something happened to me before, when, as, and if, we get married. Then you'll have a vested interest in me. In twenty years, just staying on the job, I'll have take-home pay of around fifty-five hundred dollars. If I retire, I get a pension of half that. If I get retired sooner because of injury, I get three-quarters pay. If I get killed, my wife gets a year of full pay and then a pension of one half. Not fancy, but still it's security for you."

"How dandy!" Nora exclaimed. "So I'd better cherish you till we march down the aisle together, purely from the financial point of view. You're making a strong case, Craig. Any other added inducements?"

Presently they were driving down Lafayette and past the building in which Rescue Unit Number One had its home. Here was housed a company of men rigorously trained in the business of saving lives threatened by fire or by smoke. In their big red car was every device known to the science of rescue from varieties of fog nozzles to power drills for penetrating concrete floors; from protective equipment to prevent burns or scalds, to filters which could supply breathable air for two hours in dense smoke. There would be found the more portable smoke mask. Every inch of space inside and out had been arranged to carry a maximum of devices to release penned victims and to protect firemen as they went about their business of saving lives. Here was a little, devoted company who spent their days experimenting to find more efficient ways to do their job, or to test new devices to make their work safer or to add to their efficiency in reaching and in transporting to safety imprisoned or injured persons who otherwise would die unpleasant deaths.

They continued on their way and reached the Fogarty apartment shortly after six o'clock. Nora unlocked the door and they went in, expecting to find Chief Fogarty at home, possibly enjoying an afternoon nap. But he was not there. That he had been at home was testified to by the Sunday newspaper scattered over the floor, and by an ash tray beside his favorite chair containing four cigar butts.

"Probably went for a walk," Nora said. "Read the paper while I scratch up a cold supper, if you can survive on cold roast beef and potato salad. Father'll be home by that time."

Craig seated himself in Chief Fogarty's chair and scanned the paper. The news on the front page did not interest him, but on page three was a story that gripped his attention. The dateline was Toledo, Ohio. It might have been a duplicate of the jewelry store robbery except for certain changes in scenery and costume. There had been an incendiary fire. In the excitement of this there had arrived not a red fire chief's car but a mail truck of the panel variety. This was not unusual, but what was unusual was that four

137

mailmen alighted and carried into the store two heavy bags of mail. They had awed the clerks with firearms and helped themselves to the contents of showcases and vault. They had walked out with their booty and driven away in their truck. Two frightened clerks testified that the robbers did not look human, that their faces were exactly alike and expressionless. In the confusion of the fire it was difficult to give the alarm, and precious minutes elapsed before the police were notified. Long before that the truck had disappeared as if it had been a drawing erased from a slate.

"Rubber masks again," Craig said to himself. "Otherwise the same technique."

At the tail end of the story a small boy had volunteered the information that, on east Fifty-sixth Street near the river, he had seen a large van standing by the curb with tailboard down. The boy said it was an extra-long tailboard and that a mail truck had come along and run up this ramp into the cavernous interior of the van. This had interested the lad and he had crossed the street to watch proceedings. Whereupon a mailman had jumped down, boxed his ears and told him to scram before he got hurt worse.

It appeared that the police placed little credence in this story because the boy was a well-known neighborhood imp who might even be classed as a juvenile delinquent.

"Toledo!" Craig said to himself. "They're working east. The next razzle-dazzle might be here in New York."

This apartment was as much his home as his own rooms. In it he was free to conduct himself as a son of the family. He got to his feet and walked into Uncle Paddy's bedroom and through it to the bath where he washed hands and face and brushed his hair. As he walked back through the bedroom he saw a bankbook on the floor close to Uncle Paddy's old-fashioned roll-top desk. He stooped to pick it up and replace it on the desk, and it fell open in his hand. He did not mean to snoop into Uncle Paddy's affairs, but his eyes could not help seeing the figures on the page. The book showed a balance of $25,750. A round number with no cents. It was as if he had stepped into a tank of ice water. The shock was almost physical. Where, his mind demanded, did Uncle Paddy get such a sum of money? On his salary he never could have saved such a sum. And then, ignoring the ethics of his action, he examined the bankbook from first to last entry. There were no small deposits. The least he could find was two hundred and fifty dollars—the greatest was two thousand. These sums had been deposited over a term of years.

Craig tossed the little book on the desk and sat down abruptly in the revolving chair. Was this money the cause of Uncle Paddy's strange, worried manner of late? Was this an explanation of his attitude toward the man Clyde Tupper?

His love for Uncle Paddy rejected the implications. His respect and admiration for the man who had been a father to him refused to accept the conclusion that logic indicated. His thoughts became an almost audible cry of denial. In spite of anything he refused to believe that Uncle Paddy was other than an upright man whose integrity and loyalty were beyond question. Nevertheless, this thing must be explained. Uncle Paddy must tell him where these various sums of money had come from and how he had acquired them.

He stood up and paced the room distractedly. He returned to the revolving chair and sat there, chin on chest, staring at the desk-top. Suddenly as if jolted by a high-voltage current of electricity he jerked erect and reached for one of the vertical compartments at the back of the desk. He drew from it a folder. In his period of novitiate as a marshal he had seen many duplicates of this folder. He had to make sure. The paper was old, but the legend that identified its contents was legible.

This thing, this fact, was impossible, but it was true. It was no nightmare, no hallucination. It was a solid, material, inescapable fact that he held in his hand. And that fact bade fair to topple into ruin all his ideals, his confidence in the honor of mankind, all the foundations of probity upon which his life was based.

For the file he grasped in trembling fingers was the missing file; the file that had been abstracted from the office of the Chief Fire Marshal. The file containing the reports of the investigation of that incendiary fire where his father had been murdered!

CHAPTER NINETEEN

THE SHOCK to Craig Batts was doubly appalling. It would have shaken him to his very foundations to find a bankbook with total deposits of $25,750. Somehow this might be accounted for honestly. It was within the bounds of possibility that Uncle Paddy had acquired the various deposited sums in a manner he need not be ashamed of. But the folder stolen from the fire marshal's office was not a thing that could be explained away. There it was, a stark, incriminating fact. To Craig it was all the more shocking because Uncle Paddy had been present at the fire in a subordinate capacity. He had been present at the scene of the murder and now in his possession was all the evidence collected in the investigation of that murder. The conclusion was inescapable—that Uncle Paddy feared that evidence and had procured its theft as a measure of self-protection. From that reasoning could emerge another dreadful fact: that Uncle Paddy had been concerned in the killing of Chief Batts!

And if that were true the years of kindness—the years when Chief Fogarty had stood to Craig in the place of a parent—were a series of black lies. Stemming, perhaps, from remorse.

Craig sat, gray-faced, eyes unseeing, as he strove to cope with this catastrophe. Here, then, was the hold which the man Tupper had over Chief Fogarty. Here was the guilt which, in some manner, Tupper had discovered and which he was using to impose his will. It could be Tupper himself who had supplied those sums of money in return for services rendered.

Here was a calamity which Craig must face alone. He was confronted by sworn duty which, if performed, would cause black tragedy. A life, a career, held in honor by the department and by the public, would be brought down in tragic debacle, and a public servant wearing the medal of heroism would be exposed as a taker of bribes, false to his duty, possibly as the murderer of his comrade and friend.

For the first time his tortured mind thought of Nora Fogarty and what such exposure would do to her. To his little comrade. To this beautiful, desirable woman who, in that dark instant, he realized was dearer to him than anything else on earth. A barrier would be erected between them which could never be removed or scaled. No matter what he did, no matter how he handled this situation, he would be separated from Nora forever.

It was a problem in which no logic could help. That peculiar trick mind of his could function to no purpose here. There were various paths he could follow. First, he could ignore what he had found, stand aside and let events take their course. Second, he could resign from the force and disappear. Third, he could cling coldly and exactly to his duty and lay all facts in his possession before the Chief Marshal. Those seemed to be the only choices. But then he thought of a third possibility. This possibility could not save Uncle Paddy. This possibility would bring to punishment the man who was concerned in the murder of his father, Chief Batts, but would also see to it that Chief Fogarty was not punished alone, but that the men or man who had suborned him, who had bought his loyalty and his honor, should pay as he had to pay. That he or they should be discovered and punished and made to suffer as Uncle Paddy had been made to suffer.

It was a strange thing, but he found he thought of Chief Fogarty only with sympathy. That demand for blood vengeance against the slayers of his father—which had been a compelling motive of his life, an atavism inherited down long generations from wild tribal ancestors—seemed to have lost its power. What he felt in his young heart was not rage at Uncle Paddy, but an agony sharp and deep because this thing was true of the man he had so loved and admired.

Nora's voice came through from the dining room. "Supper," she called, and her voice was a note of music. It was a magic note of music. As it sang in his ears he was conscious that something miraculous had happened to him. A weight had lifted from his mind and a grip of cold, horrid fingers had loosened their grip upon his heart.

141

It came not from reason or from logic, but from some beneficent source above and beyond human reason. . . . In spite of any ponderable, finite evidence to the contrary, he knew that Uncle Paddy was still Uncle Paddy, guiltless, admirable, of an integrity which nothing could impair. He knew it absolutely, with a certainty which nothing could ever change. And in that instant he knew the meaning of the word comfort. It was not elation. It was more gentle than elation. It was a peace such as he had never known, and in a word of prayer he expressed his gratitude that he could have faith of the sort that passed human understanding.

He replaced bankbook and folder on the desk and walked firmly into the dining room. Nora looked into his face and caught her breath.

"What is it, Craig? What has happened?" she asked.

He paused an instant before replying, and then he said softly, but with conviction, "Everything is all right, Gum Drop. . . . Everything is good. We can be at peace."

Somehow she was awed. "You speak," she said in awed tones, "and have the look as if you have seen a vision."

Before she could reply the doorbell whirred and the mood was broken. Nora went to open the door and Craig could hear her greeting the visitor.

"Why, Annie," she said. "Come in. Come in. We're just sitting down to a bit of supper."

"Is Mr. Batts here?" Annie Mertz asked. "I came in the hope of finding him."

"To be sure he's here. Come into the dining room. It's peaked you look and pale. You'd be better for a bite of food and a cup of coffee."

The girl, unsmiling, preceded Nora into the dining room and took a chair at the side of the table.

"You were wanting to see me, Annie?" Craig asked. "What can I do for you?"

"I think," she said in a low voice, "that I have information to serve you."

"That I will be glad to have. What does it concern?"

"It concerns the setting of fires," she said.

"That would be my business," he answered.

"The setting of fires for cash."

142

"That is a bad thing, Annie. And maybe a dangerous thing to know about. Is it facts you have to tell me?"

"Sure facts," she said, "that I learned by seeking and following and listening. A little girl like me, Mr. Batts, can go where no policeman could go, and hear what no policeman could hear. And there are times when tongues are loose as at no other times. And a cheap price it is to pay. For what he has done to little Fifi, I'll not be satisfied till he's behind the bars—or maybe worse."

"It's about Clyde Tupper you speak?"

"Him," Annie said. "There's to be a fire. This is the way of it. . . . It is a business, and Tupper is the head of it. As also he deals in reefers and in the numbers and other evil things."

"How do you know these things, Annie?"

"About the reefers I know because I go to jam sessions where the boys are on the beam. And because I am little Annie and well known, they talk to me. About the numbers I know because I know Broadway and the streets off Broadway and Jacobs' Beach and all."

"You could be hurt, Annie, by nosing into such matters."

"Who bothers about little Annie?" she said with a shrug. "And I do not care what happens to me if I can do a big harm to Tupper. . . . And here is how he does with fires. News he collects of businesses that lose money, or are bankrupt or need to collect insurance. And he gets word to them that a fire can be set for cash down and a share in the insurance. He makes a date at night and in a dark street, where they make a deal. And the man who wants the fire signs a paper that puts him in Tupper's hands so he'll never dare squeal."

"And future blackmail," Craig said.

"That's a part of it."

"All this may be true," said Craig, "but it is not evidence for a court."

"I came tonight," Annie said grimly, "to put you in the way of getting evidence for a court. Tonight Tupper meets a customer and I can tell you where. And I can tell you who. And you can catch him at it, and the paper signed will be your evidence."

"You're sure, Annie? You're sure of this meeting?"

"I know," she answered firmly.

And she recited the name of the customer and described his

143

factory, which was a woodworking plant in the suburbs of Brooklyn. And she named the place of meeting, which was an arch under Brooklyn Bridge which would be dark and safe for such an assignation on Sunday night.

"And the hour is ten o'clock," Annie said.

"Tupper meets this Mannheim under Brooklyn Bridge at ten to-night to complete the arrangement?" Craig asked.

"It's a big insurance," Annie said.

Craig nodded and then frowned. "I hope you've been careful, Annie. If it became known that you've been nosing and bringing information to me, it wouldn't be so good for you."

"Don't worry about me," the girl said.

Craig looked at his watch. It was a quarter after eight. "Your father's late," he said to Nora.

"Not unusual," she said. And then, "You'll be going, of course. Be careful, Craig."

"Will you let me stay here with you," Annie asked, "until we hear?"

"When I can," Craig promised, "I'll telephone."

He descended to the street and walked to the subway, which he took to Manhattan. There was ample time before the hour of the meeting. He stood at the corner where once had been the home of a great newspaper and studied the neighborhood. The streets were all but deserted. Off to his right, eerie in that gloom, rose the cables of the great bridge spanning the turbid river. Down there, toward the dark swirling water, was an unchancy area, ill-lighted, ill-smelling. He found a spot where he could stand, invisible, and command the approach to the bridge. Tupper, when he came, must walk or drive from the left, from Manhattan. He felt confident the man would come on foot, because a motorcar going down toward the water might be conspicuous—might attract the curiosity of some patrolman, especially if it were to stop and wait.

Craig glanced at his watch and found he had time on his hands. Somewhere in the night a tug whistle made its warning heard. But for the most part there was stillness, a nerve-straining stillness which can be found in a great city only on a Sabbath night. Six days of the week a million human beings milled in that region, trucks rumbled, taxicabs sounded their warnings. Six days a week men and women went about their business there, pursuing the dollar. But on this day and at this hour it spread there dead as if there had been some great exodus.

In the neighborhood of nine-thirty a dark-colored car drove past him, not rapidly, not furtively, and disappeared in the murky warren below. It was trying, this vigil. He dared not smoke, for the glow of a cigarette would give notice of his presence in the recess where he stood.

Then, when it lacked but ten minutes of the hour, a stoutish man passed within feet of where Craig lurked. He walked hurriedly, head forward on craning neck. A man going about his lawful concerns walks in a certain confident manner. He may proceed briskly or slowly. He may make haste or he may dawdle as if he had time on his hands. But there will be something honest in his manner. But a man whose affairs are not above suspicion will not bear himself in that manner. He will be aware of his own purpose and he will not welcome the gaze of passers-by. A guilty conscience will cause him to glance over his shoulder and to look shiftily from side to side. There will, especially in a deserted spot such as this, be almost an odor of fear.

Craig's keen eyes appraised the heavy-set man and was aware of furtiveness. The man proceeded for a distance, paused, and the sound of his footsteps ceased. Then he crossed the street toward the bridge and the arches under the bridge. After which there were only silence and nothingness.

Craig waited, for he was sure that the man who had passed was he who came to meet and to reach a criminal agreement with Tupper. He was sure this was the man Mannheim who came to suborn arson and, perforce, to put himself forever in the sinister power of Tupper.

Craig remained motionless for what seemed to him hours, but was only a minute. Then he crossed the street, and, walking soundlessly, keeping to the darkest of the shadows, made his way toward the rendezvous. A hundred feet, two hundred feet he made his way silent as a shadow. As he proceeded he went more slowly, more stealthily, pausing every few paces to listen.

Then he heard the muted murmur of voices and halted. Instinctively he timed himself, and only then did he feel his aloneness and the inadequacy of being alone. Suddenly he realized that he had not done well. That he had acted brashly, improperly, rashly, to undertake this mission by himself without alerting the Fire Marshal's office and procuring adequate assistance. He was culpable, and now nothing but success could justify him.

He had no fear of the man Mannheim, but Tupper was an antagonist of another color. Tupper would not submit tamely to arrest. But there was nothing for it now but to make the effort. But even so that effort must not be made until the evidence was ready —until Mannheim had signed that criminal agreement with Tupper which put in writing the terms of the agreement. Until there was completed a document which would be proof positive of guilt in any court in the land.

Craig lurked, only feet from the pair whose murmuring voices fell silent. There was light. Tupper had caused a small electric torch to glow, and its beam was directed upon a white paper and upon a hand holding a fountain pen. The hand and pen moved. The document was signed by the victim.

Craig prepared to move, to pounce, to take advantage of surprise and so to make good the arrest before Tupper could offer resistance. He poised on the balls of his feet, muscles tense. He was sure of himself, and a certain elation glowed.

He was about to launch himself when headlights from the direction of the river rushed toward them, making all as bright as day. Craig drew back out of the oncoming glare. There was the squeal of tortured tires as the car skidded to a stop. From it leaped three men, and in the hands of the first was a gun of the variety known to gangsters as a tommy gun. A peremptory voice said, "Hold it! . . . Reach!"

Two other men darted across the walk. The arm of one rose and fell, and a sap descended upon Mannheim's skull. He slumped to the pavement. Tupper had uttered no sound. He stood as though confounded. A gun was thrust against his spine and the peremptory voice commanded him to get into the car. He obeyed, daring to make no protest. There was the sound of meshing gears and the car sped away with its prisoner.

The man Mannheim lay where he had fallen, as if of no account. He was simply left to lie there disregarded as if he were of no consequence. Craig, bewildered by what had taken place, bent over the man and lifted his head. Mannheim moaned. There was a trickle of blood. He breathed shallowly and then breathing seemed to cease completely.

Craig had a prisoner, but the prisoner seemed likely to be of little good to him. One thing was clear. He must get assistance. Mannheim must have medical attention if a spark of life remained. There was no danger of his escaping. Craig eased him as best he could and ran toward the bridge approach. And as he ran he remembered two things that his trick mind had seen and remembered. The first of these was that the faces of the abductors had a strange, inhuman look. Such a look as would be present if the men wore skin-tight rubber masks. The other remembered thing was that under the rear of the car had been a hitch—such a connection as was used to attach a trailer.

CHAPTER TWENTY

IT WAS Craig's good fortune to find a prowl car within a few minutes. He identified himself and an ambulance was summoned which carried Mannheim to Bellevue Hospital. From there he belatedly reported to headquarters and was directed to come in immediately. Twenty minutes after he arrived in the Municipal Building the Chief Fire Marshal came storming in, and on his heels Lieutenant of Detectives Fisano. The Chief occupied his chair behind his flat-topped desk; the detective tilted a chair against the wall and both of them glared at Craig. Craig was not happy. He knew the sensations of a culprit about to receive sentence.

"I could," growled the Chief Marshal, "suspend you and prefer charges."

"Yes, sir," said Craig.

"Give reason why I shouldn't," snapped the Chief. "Was your idea to grab glory and see your name in the headlines?"

"It was not that, sir," Craig answered. "I never thought of that."

"You never thought," amended the Chief. "We'll consider your case in due time. Commence now at the beginning. Leave nothing out."

Craig, in formal language, told of the coming of Annie Mertz to the Fogarty apartment and of her disclosures. He described his journey to Brooklyn Bridge and his wait there near the place of rendezvous. He described the coming of Mannheim and the arrival of Tupper. Vividly he told his hearers how he had stealthily approached the two men, had seen Mannheim affix his signature to a paper.

148

"I moved, sir, to take them into custody when this automobile with its headlights full on came out of the darkness and stopped at the curb. Three men got out, one with a tommy gun. One man sapped Mannheim; the other two forced Tupper into the car, and they were off at full speed."

"While," snapped the Chief, "you stood like a dummy."

"Sir," said Craig respectfully, "it was done so fast and so efficiently that they would have gotten away with it if there had been a dozen of me."

"What then?"

"I left Mannheim and found a prowl car, and we called an ambulance and he was taken to Bellevue. From there I reported."

"How ever did you think of that?" the Chief asked witheringly. "And that is all?"

"There is more, sir," Craig said.

"Such as what?"

"Two things," Craig answered. "The three men wore rubber masks."

The Chief and Fisano exchanged glances. "You are sure?"

"Certain," said Craig. "And the car was the same that carried the robbers away from the jewelry store holdup."

"What's that?"

"Same make. Under the rear was a hitch for attaching a trailer."

"Now why," asked the Chief, frowning at his folded hands, "would these rubber mask boys have snatched Tupper?"

"I would reason, sir, that Tupper is retail and the masked people are wholesale. They wanted to eliminate competition. It could be, sir, that Tupper, with his connections, was learning too much."

"Sounds probable," Fisano agreed.

"But," Craig said slowly, hesitating as if waiting for permission to speak.

"Go ahead, young man," said the Chief.

"I think, sir, the really important thing about it all is that the next fire and robbery are to be in New York. We believe, don't we, Chief, that this gang travels fast about the country? In a trailer. So the presence in town of this tow car with a trailer hitch would mean that the trailer is here, with the gang living in it. The next job will be in New York City."

149

"The little birdie didn't tell you when and where?" asked the Chief ironically.

Fisano intervened. "I agree with the young man, Chief."

"Agree with him! The facts speak for themselves."

"Right," answered Fisano. "But it was this young man who discovered the facts."

"I'll run my department," growled the Chief. And then, less rigorously, "It will be remembered in his favor. But it's a nice howdy-do! It's a dandy mess he lays in our laps. Here we sit, knowing there is an incendiary fire planned, under cover of which a crime will be committed. Nice situation. Hanging over our heads, and we as helpless as so many babies in a nursery!"

"This," Lieutenant Fisano said heavily, "is going to be pretty grim, sitting around waiting for it to strike."

"Knowing," agreed the Chief, "that it is coming and not being able to do a thing to prevent it. Anywhere in Manhattan, Queens, the Bronx or Richmond!"

"But," said Fisano, "knowing what is coming, we can take precautions."

"What precautions?"

"We can treat every fire alarm as if this was it," Fisano said, "and throw a cordon of police and marshals around it."

The Chief Marshal snorted. "How many fires did we answer in 1956?" he demanded.

"No idea."

"Forty-nine thousand, five hundred and eleven," the Chief Marshal told him. "Just where'll we get cops and marshals to seal off that many fires? That's a hundred and thirty-five a day on the average. The whole United States Army and Navy couldn't handle it."

"But, sir, we can eliminate most alarms," Craig pointed out.

"How?" demanded the Chief gruffly.

"Every one of these fires and robberies around the country," Craig said, "has been next to or across the street from a bank or a jewelry store."

"Batts is right about that, Chief," Fisano said.

"There aren't so many important jewelry stores," Craig said, "that would be worth while looting."

"But banks and branch banks," Fisano said. "They're scattered all over town."

"When can this Mannheim be questioned?" Fisano asked.

"Concussion. Anybody's guess when he'll come out of it."

"And when he talks," Craig said, "all he can sing about is Tupper and his torches. He'll know nothing that can help with this bigger business. . . . Tupper might, if we could lay hands on him. Of course he might have been snatched merely to eliminate competition. But more likely it was because he had got to know too much."

"In which case," the Chief said, "we'll find him like we found William Tecumseh Peabody—full of holes."

"Could it be a pattern?" Craig asked.

"What kind of a pattern?" asked the Chief Marshal.

"Well, sir, these fires and robberies have been so similar—an incendiary fire near the place that is to be robbed. Then, arriving in the confusion in a counterfeit fire department car, or police department car, or some other vehicle of a public nature, are three or four men in rubber masks. All the same technique, directed by a mind that is in a rut, that puts faith in repetition."

"So what of it?" asked the Chief Marshal.

"That directing mind would work the same in other matters. There was William Tecumseh Peabody. First he was snatched and held prisoner. He wasn't killed until he tried to make his escape. Tupper has been snatched and will be held prisoner. Otherwise, why not scrag him under Brooklyn Bridge and leave him lying there? Maybe, sir, the boss of this business has a prejudice against murder and kills only when it's absolutely necessary."

Both police lieutenant and Chief Marshal sat silent and thoughtful. Then Fisano nodded. "Could be. Could be part of a picture of the man emerges. A man with a mind that runs in a rut, and a man with compunctions against killing."

"Possibly," said Craig, "a man with a mental thing. Maybe a firebug, but a firebug who isn't satisfied with just setting fires. Let's lay out the facts we have in a row."

"Go ahead," directed the Chief.

"The outstanding facts," Craig said, "are the murder of Peabody. And the finding of those uniforms and masks in his house. And the setting fire to his residence. And the fact that he knew or thought he knew the guilty person. And that he believed—or hoped—that

151

guilty person was insane. Because he consulted a mental specialist about him. Which, it seems to me, sir, indicates that the criminal might be a friend of Peabody's, moving in the same social stratum, living ostensibly a blameless or even distinguished life."

"It's bad enough," growled the Chief, "without your fancying it up."

"The indications," Fisano said, "are that it's pretty fancy."

And complicated, thought Craig, though he did not put the thought into words for the others to hear, by Chief Fogarty and his dealings with Tupper—whatever they were. And by the possession by Uncle Paddy of a bankbook with deposits of $25,750. And by the presence in Uncle Paddy's desk of that folder stolen from the fire marshal's files containing the reports on the incendiary blaze in which Craig's father had met his death.

Someone in a position of trust in the department had stolen that file. It could not have been Uncle Paddy himself, for he never had been in the office nor, had he come there, could he have had access to the files without arousing attention. Either a member of the corps of assistant marshals had committed the theft, or some other individual who could come and go in those offices without attracting attention.

Craig held firmly to his certainty that Uncle Paddy's rectitude was beyond question, which left the troubling question of how that envelope of papers reached his desk. Craig did not lose sight of the possibility that it had been planted there. If so it had been done either by the unidentified head man of the nationwide arson conspiracy, or by Tupper. More likely Tupper, who seemed to have some sort of hold upon the old Chief.

"If," said the Chief Marshal unhappily, "the newspapers and the public get wind of this, we'll have hornets buzzing around our ears."

"I don't see how we can help it," Fisano said. "The police department will have to be alerted, and so will the fire department. The newspaper boys will have it five minutes after. And there we are."

"And a pretty picture it will make. We, sitting on our behinds, knowing a major crime is going to be committed, and helpless to do a damn thing about it."

"Sword of Damocles," said Craig.

"Who of which?" demanded the Chief.

152

"Just a classical allusion," Craig said uncomfortably.

"Ain't things bad enough," demanded the Chief, "without lugging in Greeks and Romans? We got enough of them running restaurants and spaghetti joints in New York without dragging in their great-great granddaddies. . . . We can get no farther by gabbin'," he said. "Break it up now and get on the job."

As they arose the Chief glowered at Craig. "Bear in mind," he said ominously, "that you ain't a one-man Bureau of Fire Investigation. We haven't much use for a lad that says never mind the signals, just let me carry the ball."

"Yes, sir," said Craig, flushing and hoping that this barb would be the worst punishment he would suffer.

Nearly every desk in the two rooms occupied by the assistant fire marshals was in use, and pens scratched busily on reports. Luke Priddy at the desk touching Craig Batts's looked up quizzically and asked in his rather metallic, monotonous voice, "Any skin left?"

"Barely enough to cover my bones," Craig answered.

"Lucky you didn't get clobbered," Priddy said. "You might be in Bellevue instead of this Mannheim."

"Right you are," admitted Craig.

"Where'll you be if he refuses to talk?" Priddy asked.

"Up the creek without a bucket," Craig answered ruefully.

"He won't talk," Priddy said positively. "Fifth Amendment! First thing he was told when negotiations started. Also he'll have been told what'll happen to him if he does spill."

"Could be."

"Anyhow, good luck."

"I'll need it."

"And don't forget that seventeen members of the department were killed in line of duty last year."

The Deputy Chief signaled from his door for Craig, and Craig entered his small, glass-partitioned office.

"You are to meet Detective Lieutenant Fisano in the entrance to the building where Tupper has his offices," the Deputy Chief ordered. "He has a search warrant."

Craig descended to the ground floor and walked to the subway. Fisano was waiting for him in the corridor by the newsstand where Tupper had knocked him down in their one physical encounter. They rode up to Tupper's floor, and Fisano produced a key to

153

admit them to the office. One glance at the reception room wa
enough to tell them that someone had been before them. The office
were a shambles. Every drawer in the desk had been jerked out an
its contents strewed over the floor. Pictures and calendars had bee
ripped from the walls, furniture had been upended. In Tupper'
private office the havoc was even greater. There it seemed as if spit
had animated the searcher. Upholstery had been slashed to ribbons
drawers not only had been pulled from the desk but it seemed the
had been kicked and trampled in an avid desire to damage. It wa
the same in Tupper's living apartment. It was as though som
maniac obsessed by an impulse to wreak havoc had given ful
reign to his disordered mind.

"If," Fisano said, surveying the ruin ruefully, "there's anything
left for us, you can have it. An earthquake or a cyclone couldn'
have done a more thorough job."

"It's—it's extravagant," Craig said, struggling for a word to fit
"But it's systematic. Madness with a method."

"We've had everything in this case but a lunatic at large."

"Maybe, Lieutenant, we even have that."

"Look at this!" exclaimed Fisano. He picked up the remains o
an expensive wastebasket that had been stomped into a scarcely
recognizable mass of bits and splinters. "No reason for that excep
malice."

In all that Craig had observed since his first contact with thi
case there had been only efficiency; evidence of sane planning; o
the direction of an astute brain. Perhaps a mind that operated in a
rut, but a rut that brought results. Here was the only evidence o
disorder. He thought of that report to William Tecumseh Peabody
from the mental expert. He wondered how that report would have
read could this symptom be added to the data.

"However crazy this bird may have been," he said to Fisano, "he
did a systematic job of searching. If anything was hidden here i
was found."

He leaned against the wall and stared at the room and the chaos
of it. It was as if that observant mind of his were determined to
wrest some secret from the confusion; to piece together a jigsaw puzzle picture from the fragments.

"I don't believe he was searching for some definite thing," he
said presently. "He was hunting on speculation."

He got away from his position against the wall and walked to the open bathroom door. Here in the washbasin was a toothbrush whose handle had been snapped and the fragments of a glass. He peered down at them, and something was not right. He picked out and tossed away the pieces of the toothbrush, but did not disturb the shards of glass. Then he nodded his head and stirred them with a cautious finger. Fisano watched him intently. Craig, between thumb and finger, selected a bit of glass roughly triangular in shape and half an inch long.

"Thought so," he said to himself.

"Thought what?" asked Fisano.

"That something didn't belong." He held up the bit of glass. "Different kind of glass. Thinner." He shook his head. "It shone different. You could notice it."

"I didn't," Fisano said.

"No," said Craig abstractedly. "No. . . . I just kind of notice things."

"So what more do you notice?"

"I'd guess," said Craig, "that the fellow who busted the glass dropped his spectacles in the bowl and broke them. He picked out all the pieces but this. Funny a man would drop his glasses if he was wearing them. Most glasses hang on."

"Well," said Fisano, "no use hanging around here."

"No use," said Craig abstractedly. "No use at all."

Fisano locked the door behind them and they descended to the lobby. The man behind the cigar counter peered at Craig, recognized him and grinned derisively. "Win any fights lately?" he jeered.

"You'd be surprised," Craig said mildly. And then to the detective, "Rimless eyeglasses," he said.

CHAPTER TWENTY-ONE

CRAIG looked up from his desk as two men passed down the aisle toward the filing cabinets against the wall. One of them was the Deputy Chief Fire Marshal, the other was Pieter Van Rensselaer. The dapper little gentleman was complete with malacca cane, spats, black Homburg, glove on his left hand, handkerchief's corner correctly peeping from his jacket pocket. He caught Craig's eye and nodded in the manner of the lord of the manor greeting a tenant on his estate. There was, Craig noted, a sudden line between the little gentleman's eyes as if he were displeased at something. He stopped and seemed to find it necessary to explain his presence. At this Craig wondered because he could see no reason why Van Rensselaer should account for himself in that place.

"Ah," he said. "Ah, Mr. Batts, is it not? Of course. Of course. Eyesight not so good. Not so good. Commissioner graciously given me access to the files. History of the department. My avocation. Have spent many hours in the library in Long Island City. Remarkable. Labor of love. But history would be far from complete without chapter on incendiary fires, eh?"

"Indeed not," agreed Craig.

"Have found these reports of investigations highly interesting. Great efficiency. Originality. Great ingenuity. Yes. Yes. . . . Ah. Yes."

Having delivered himself thus, the impeccable gentleman passed along to the files.

"King of the buffs!" said the marshal at the desk behind Craig.

156

"Hope he lives to finish this book. Been working on it years to my knowledge."

"Does he consult these files often?" Craig asked.

"When he wants to. Got the run of the place."

"Got all his buttons?" Craig asked.

"If you ask me they're all hanging by a thread. What he's got is better than buttons. He's first cousin to every bloomin' top-drawer family in New York. But—what I hear—he's a smart old hombre. Just nuts about fires."

Craig finished his paper work and went out on his day's assignment, which was to go to the home of William Tecumseh Peabody and re-examine its caretaker Soapy Japes. Before the doors of the elevator clanged shut Mr. Van Rensselaer stepped sprightly into the cage, blinked to Craig and said, "Ah. Ah, we meet again."

Craig studied the man covertly. Something attracted his scrutiny, or rather the lack of something. Craig sensed an absence, but it was not until the cage stopped at the ground floor that he identified the missing thing. It was the monocle.

"Are you bound uptown, Mr. Batts?" Van Rensselaer asked in a formal voice.

"I am," Craig told him.

"Then perhaps we may share a cab. I myself am traveling as far north as Forty-ninth Street."

"It will be a pleasure, sir," Batts said.

It was some minutes before a cab came along. Craig's companion seemed averse to conversation, but stood swinging his stick jauntily and eying each passing woman with calculating eye. More than one eyed him and smiled with amusement to see such an anachronism walking the streets. But Pieter preened himself, aware only of the attention he attracted but mistaking the reason for it.

"Even at my age," he said smugly to Craig, "you will note that I do not pass unnoticed by the ladies. Gratifying."

"It is indeed," said Craig, unsmiling.

A cab swung to the curb. Van Rensselaer opened the door with a gesture and bowed Craig to enter. *"Monsieur!"* he said grandly. And then, when Craig was safely inside, he nodded his head stiffly and said, "Myself!"

Scarcely a word was exchanged during the ride uptown. The little man seemed distrait, and Craig himself had things to busy his mind. The cab was directed to stop at the corner of the Avenue of the Americas and Forty-ninth Street. Van Rensselaer bent forward to look at the meter, which read a dollar and twenty cents.

"That," he said to Craig, "will be sixty cents apiece. Plus the tip, of course. I never tip more than the exact 10 per cent. That is twelve cents." He fumbled in his pocket and placed the exact sum of sixty-six cents in Craig's palm. "I always share a cab when possible. A penny saved is a penny earned."

Craig paid and dismissed the cab. His companion pointedly said good-by and trotted away, swinging his cane. Craig stood looking after him a moment and, on impulse, followed eastward. His quarry crossed Fifth Avenue and a block beyond turned to the right. Then a block or so farther north he turned to the left toward Fifth Avenue again. Now he walked very slowly and seemed to be studiously observant. He seemed, or so it appeared to Craig, to be committing the buildings facing upon the street to memory. Every now and then he slackened his pace or even halted for a second. He paused markedly to admire the architecture of the uptown branch of the Merchants and Miners National Bank. He crossed the street to enter its handsome bronze doors. Craig, more than interested now, followed in his tracks and peered into the interior. Van Rensselaer stood at a desk filling out a check, which he proceeded to cash. Craig withdrew and retired into a doorway down the street. Van Rensselaer emerged and resumed his stroll toward Fifth Avenue.

It had been curious behavior, but then it had been an eccentric individual who performed it. Craig abandoned the pursuit. Something told him there would be nothing else interesting to see. But as he turned and bent his steps in the direction of the Peabody residence, he said to himself, "If that wasn't a guaranteed member of one of the first families, I'd say he was casing the joint."

He continued on his way to the Peabody residence, where he descended into the area and rang the bell of the service entrance. In a moment Soapy Japes's face drew aside the curtain and peered out. With splendid gravity he opened the door and received Craig with trained decorum.

"Good day, sir. May I be of service?"

"Just dropped around to visit," Craig told him.

"Very gratifying, if I may say so, sir. If your visit is official, I will take you to the library. If it is a social call upon myself, the kitchen would be more suitable."

"If," said Craig, "there's a cup of coffee, I vote for the kitchen."

While the percolator bubbled and gurgled, the two men sat with the table between them and talked about William Tecumseh Peabody and his virtues and foibles, his habits and his aberrations. What Craig was seeking was some indication of the identity of the individual into whose sanity Mr. Peabody had been making investigations. But Soapy was unable to enlighten him.

"When you were a confidence man and before the days of your reformation," Craig said, "you were rated a shrewd judge of character."

"Indeed I was, sir. It was an important asset."

"Right. Then cast your mind over such friends as Mr. Peabody was most intimate with. Which one of them, appraising them with your old criminal eye, would you say had the best qualification to be a crook?"

"The individual with highest qualification to be an able criminal," Soapy said, "would be he who most efficiently conceals those attributes. I owed my own success to my ability to present to the world an impeccable character. In short, to assume characteristics least apt to create any iota of suspicion."

"Yes."

"If my profession were that of a confidence man," Soapy said, "I would seem to the world to be most gullible. If I aspired to be a peterman, sir, I would build for myself a reputation for being excessively afraid of explosives. My fear would be an obsession so that I studied about them and dragged them into conversations. And so on, sir, through the various branches of crime."

"You would advertise yourself as the opposite of what you are?"

"Succinctly put, sir."

Craig finished his cup of coffee and kicked back his chair. He extended a hand to Soapy, who hesitated an instant before he took it, as if making up his mind whether it would be seemly for him to do so.

"Obliged to you," Craig told him sincerely. "Why don't you write a textbook on the psychology of crime?"

"I will consider it, sir. Whether it would be suitable for me to aspire so high."

159

He showed Craig out of the area door. The young man made his way by the shortest route to the subway and rode impatiently to Brooklyn, alighting at the entrance nearest to the Fogarty apartment. Nora answered his ring and was surprised to see him at that hour of the day.

"It's business, Gingerbread," he said gravely. "I want to look at Uncle Paddy's desk."

"At Father's desk? Why?"

"For his good, I hope. But I've got to snoop."

"This is a thing to ask!" she said, coldness in her voice.

"Could anything make you believe your father is guilty of a crime, or of conniving at a crime?"

"Nothing," she replied, biting off the word.

"The same with me," he said. "You must believe that."

Her voice softened. "Yes, Craig," she said.

"In the face of any evidence to the contrary," he said gravely.

"It would be lying evidence," she said sturdily.

"In his desk is bad evidence. I've got to examine it. How it got there I don't know. You must let me see it. There's a bankbook showing he has a large sum deposited to his name. I don't care about that. But there is a folder, a file that was stolen from the records in the Fire Marshal's office. The record of the investigation into the fire during which my father was murdered."

"In my father's desk!"

"I have seen it," he said.

"Come," she said sharply.

The file was there where he had seen it on his previous visit. He sat down in Uncle Paddy's chair and, commencing at the first page, read it through to the end. Nora stood tense at his side. Her cheeks were ashen. Her little hands clenched into fists. She did not read over his shoulder, but waited with a grimness that was unnatural.

Craig read the record again, pausing now and then to concentrate upon some word or paragraph. Facts that never had been related to him made their appearance. It had been Uncle Paddy who, at frightful risk to himself, had carried Chief Batts's body out of that furnace. The Chief had not died from flames or heat of fumes, but from a bullet fired from a .32-caliber revolver. It had been a multiple fire, and the combustible had been gasoline ignited by a time fuse.

The evidence of twenty witnesses examined by police and fire marshals was preserved there. He took no notes. His peculiar memory absorbed the facts and printed them indelibly page by page. It was a visual memory. A year from now he could see those pages and read them as if the manuscript were before his eyes. The facts important to him were obscure, buried. At the time of writing them they meant nothing to any investigator; but to Craig, when fitted into the pattern he had been knitting together, they were conclusive. But before they could be used as evidence to convict, there still remained concrete facts to be adduced. It was one thing to know; it was another thing to prove to twelve good men and true.

"Sugar Bun," he said to Nora with gravity, "I think we're creeping up on the blowoff. I'm sure I know what was between Clyde Tupper and your father. I think I know what lay heavy on Uncle Paddy's heart. But these things are conclusions I have jumped to. Across gaps. I've got to fill in those gaps so the dullest mind can walk across them."

"But how—how, Craig, did this record get in Father's desk? And where did that money deposited in the bank come from?"

"I would guess," Craig said, "that the folder came by mail. As for the money, we'll let Uncle Paddy tell us about it when he's of a mind to talk."

"Craig, you made one mistake. You went alone to that secret meeting between Tupper and the man who was hiring him to burn his factory. Don't make another mistake like that. Don't be too self-sufficient. Tell the Chief Marshal everything you know or surmise. Let him take it from there. Don't carry the ball yourself with nobody calling signals. It's team play that wins."

He nodded, but did not convince her he would follow her advice.

"Craig," she said, and placed a hand on his arm to hold him, "you're smart. Maybe you're almost a genius. You've a mind that does tricks. But, boy, stop and think. There's a big difference between smartness or even genius and wisdom. One is showy and fancy; the other plods but doesn't make mistakes. I don't want to be boastful, lad, but it's myself has the wisdom. So heed me."

He peered down at her a moment, and at first she thought he was offended with her plain speaking, or that his vanity, of which he had a plenty, was injured. But at the end of seconds he grinned broadly and took her face between his palms.

"I'll not be kissing you now, Sugar Plum, nor speaking the words that come bubbling up into my throat, for it is not the time or place for it. But this I will declare to you: that if we shall ever come together we'll be an unbeatable pair."

"In words my grandmither would have spoke—there's no doubt but you're a broth of a boy." But instantly her face darkened and her eyes became deepest, darkest blue. "Of a sudden," she said, "something lays heavy on me. Like a black storm was impending. It's not wisdom that warns me, but something strange that should be heeded."

He was impressed. A hand reached out from the distant past when men believed in the Little People, and heard the wail of the banshee, and put faith in wise women and those to whom came the second sight.

"What would you have me do?" he asked, and awe rested heavily upon him.

"I would have you stay here behind a locked door. I would have you telephone your chief and tell him, word by word, what you know and what you believe. And tell him I am sore afraid for you and to send men to come for you in a car that you take no harm."

"He would laugh at me and call me a coward."

"He will do no such thing. Shall you call him, or must I do it myself?"

"At least I will lay all before him and ask his advice."

"And that," said a muffled voice from the doorway, "you will not do. But something different."

Startled, they turned to stare with wide eyes at the pair who stood in the bedroom door. About them was a look that was unnatural, not human. Theirs were expressionless faces, strangely pink and white. Instantly Craig knew he was seeing again men who wore rubber masks.

"You have been sent for," said one of the men in a voice that was not discourteous. "You are wanted. Miss Fogarty, I regret that I must include you." He motioned with the automatic in his hand.

With an instinctive gesture Craig swept Nora behind him, interposing himself between the girl and the two intruders. He did not have time to think it queer or admirable that, in this sudden emergency, he should not be afraid, and that his mind continued to function coolly and efficiently. In an instant he assayed the situation and its possibilities and its perils. His mind darted outside the confines of this room and this apartment and leaped gaps to a conclusion. These men had not been sent to snatch himself as other similar men had been sent to snatch Clyde Tupper. They had come for him specifically because he had become an immediate threat to their plans, and because the hour for putting those plans into execution was imminent. He, Craig Batts, must be gotten out of the way now so that he could not interfere with or frustrate the raid that was projected. And if this were true, it was proof to him that his activities had alarmed the arsonists and robbers to a point where they considered him an imminent peril.

One of the intruders stood in the doorway; the other to the right of it. Craig stood six feet away, physically relaxed but mentally tense and alert.

"Sent for?" he said. "Who sends for me?"

"Silly question," answered the man. And then, in a reasonable tone of voice, "Listen, Batts, you've got to be a nuisance. But nobody's going to hurt you if you don't ask for it. Just come along like a little lamb, and in a couple of days you'll be turned loose. You and Miss Fogarty."

"That," Craig said, "I don't believe. . . . How about a deal?"

"What deal? You're in no position to propose a deal."

"I think I am," Craig said. "Leave Miss Fogarty out of this. She knows nothing. She can be no danger to you. Tie her up, if you like, and leave her here. I'll go along without a battle. But if you insist on dragging her along—"

"So what then?" asked the second man, speaking for the first time.

"Why," Craig said, "you're going to do me in anyhow. You've got to, haven't you? Well, I'll make you kill me right here, which will toss a monkey wrench into the machinery."

"Now, Batts," said the first man, "we're not amateurs. You're just talking to gain time. What for? Come along with us and you've got a chance. Make us handle the thing here and you're dead. Period. And, necessarily, Miss Fogarty."

The man in the doorway was holding his gun waist-high and ready. The second man displayed no weapon. Craig allowed his shoulders to sag and made a hopeless gesture with his hands. His voice had lost its assurance when he spoke. "Well, Nora," he said a bit tremulously, "I tried my best. We'll go peaceful," he said, "for I can do no more."

He shuffled forward a step as if the starch had gone out of him. The man in the doorway with the gun in his hand made a mistake which no professional should be guilty of. He allowed Craig to come too close to him. . . . There is a thing which all well-trained officers of the law whether they be FBI, Secret Service or properly instructed officers of the police are taught. And that is that there must intervene between realization and action a brief space of time. There is an interval between intention to shoot and sending the message to the trigger finger. Therefore the instructed gunman never allows his victim to come within arm's reach. But so cowed did Craig seem that this gunman forgot the cardinal rule. When almost chest to chest, when the second came when Craig would pass the man in the rubber mask to go through the door, his left hand chopped downward against the man's wrist, half turning him around. And with the same twisting movement his right fist smashed into the man's torso where was the solar plexus. Then, before the instant of surprise could pass, he pivoted on his heel, swinging the back of his fist against the second man's Adam's apple, fortunately missing the jaw.

"Run," he said peremptorily to Nora. "Run."

She obeyed. She flew to the outer door. Craig, not pausing to investigate the state of the intruders, but hearing sounds of choking and retching that gave him to know his blows had been effective, followed her out of the apartment and down the stairs to the street.

"Telephone," he panted.

"Drugstore on the corner," she said, equally breathless, trying to keep up with him, and striving at the same time to speak certain words which he heard only vaguely, but which seemed to be couched in old-time brogue and to be something about a broth of a boy.

CHAPTER TWENTY-TWO

CRAIG went into the booth to report to the Chief Fire Marshal's office. Nora stood near the door watching the front of the apartment house where she lived. Before Craig finished his telephoning two men came out of the building and got into a car that stood at the curb a little distance from the entrance. One of them seemed in considerable distress. They drove away with haste. When Craig came out of the booth she told him what she had seen.

"We're to stay put," he told her. "The Chief's on his way."

In far less time than would have been deemed possible the Chief's car, driven by his aide, lashed up to the corner and stopped. In the rear seat were the Chief Fire Marshal and Lieutenant Fisano. The Chief was not in good humor.

"So what have you stepped into here?" he demanded. "And what were you doing here anyway?"

"I rode uptown with Mr. Van Rensselaer," Craig said in an official voice. "When I left him I went to the home of William Tecumseh Peabody to interview Soapy Japes. When I was through with him I came here to Chief Fogarty's apartment."

"Why?"

"To examine the contents of Chief Fogarty's desk," Craig answered.

"That," grated the Chief, "requires explanation—and a good one."

"Yes, sir. By chance, sir, I found the other day in that desk a bankbook with deposits of more than twenty-five thousand dollars. And also the missing file of the investigation into the fire where my father was killed."

"You found these things in Chief Fogarty's desk. And did not report the finding to me."

"I needed to think, sir."

"So you needed to think! And what was the result of your thinking?"

"That, no matter what I found and no matter what seemed to be indicated, Uncle Paddy was an honest man, and that there was an explanation that would not discredit him."

"So you concealed evidence. You acted as judge and jury. And you acquitted Chief Fogarty."

There was a softening in the glare of the Chief's fierce eyes, though Craig was too disturbed to notice it.

"We will go into that further," the Chief said. "But fir-r-st what then happened?"

"Two armed men wearing rubber masks surprised me, sir. They were intending to kidnap me and Miss Fogarty. We managed to get away from them, sir, and I telephoned you. In the meantime the two men escaped in a car."

"I would speak a word," Nora interjected. "Assistant Fire Marshal Batts," she said, "stood in the doorway. There were two men with unnatural faces. One held a gun almost against Marshal Batts's body. The other stood ready. What followed was too quick for me to see, but both men were on the floor and Marshal Batts ordered me to run, which I did. We reached the street in safety." She paused an instant and then spoke with sudden fire. "And it's proud of him you should be instead of giving him the rough side of your tongue."

"Say you so, Miss Fogarty? And maybe I should put you in charge of the discipline of the department."

"You could go farther and do worse," she said unyieldingly.

"We will go to the apartment," said the Chief noncommittally, and Lieutenant Fisano's eyes traveled from Craig to Nora and twinkled with amusement. Few people faced up to the Chief Marshal as this girl had done and survived it so well as she.

They crossed the street and climbed the stairs. The door of the apartment stood open. The living room had not been disturbed, but the desk in Chief Fogarty's bedroom had been ransacked. The folder of the investigation was gone, but the bankbook lay on the floor among other papers. The Chief growled, "So whatever that file could have told us has been lost."

"No, sir," Craig said. "It is in my mind. At need I can recite it to you."

"What else can you recite?" demanded the Chief.

"Why," asked Lieutenant Fisano, "did they come for you?"

"One of them said I had become a nuisance," Craig answered. "It was necessary for them to get me out of the way for a little while."

"Ah, a little while."

"Why not let you have it?" asked the Chief.

Craig's eyes narrowed in thought. He concentrated. "Because," he said slowly, "their boss man has a thing against murder, if he can avoid it. And because I had to be gotten out of the way for only a short time."

"Go on," prompted Fisano.

"We believe," Craig said, "that the next raid of this gang will be in New York City. This means that it will be soon. Tomorrow maybe. I'm trying to figure why, all of a sudden, I've become such a nuisance."

"Could it be," Fisano asked, "because you saw Clyde Tupper snatched Sunday night?"

"Who knows I saw that?" Craig answered. "Nobody but the police and members of the Fire Marshal's department. . . . There could have been a leak."

"Possible," growled the Chief Marshal.

"It wasn't a member of the detective force that abstracted that folder from your files, Chief," Fisano said with raised brows.

The Chief Marshal was in a rage. Not against Fisano, but at the thought that a member of his Bureau might be guilty of treachery. But he was compelled to admit the possibility of it.

"Chief," Craig said tensely, "that folder was not removed from the files by a member of this gang. It was taken by someone who delivered it to Tupper. Who had it sent to Chief Fogarty. Tupper's office was searched for it. Chief Fogarty! This William Tecumseh Peabody was killed because he was trying to reach Chief Fogarty. Why Chief Fogarty? It seems silly, Chief, but I think it was because Chief Fogarty, when he was a boy, played on a baseball team with William Tecumseh Peabody."

"The boy has lost his mind," the Chief said to Fisano.

"It might be a good thing if some of us lost our minds the same

167

way," Fisano said with a grin. "He's the only one of us that seems to be getting any place."

"Chief," Craig said suddenly, almost as if unexpectedly to himself, "could you arrange for a three-bagger false alarm?"

"Now I know you're loopy," the Chief rumbled. "But what's the idea?"

"We don't want a real fire, do we, sir? An incendiary fire that might spread and do great damage in the heart of town?"

"Of course we don't."

"But," Craig said slowly, "they can't commit a robbery without the cover of a fire. It's the way they work. It's their pattern."

"Right, boy," said Fisano. "What are you getting at?"

"If their fire doesn't come off, they won't dare to raid the bank," Craig said in a distrait, almost dreamy manner.

"What bank?" snapped the Chief Marshal.

"Why," said Craig, his voice suddenly strong and certain, "the Merchants and Miners National Bank, sir."

The Chief and Lieutenant Fisano gaped at each other and then bent forward to stare at Craig as if he had jerked a white elephant out of a derby hat.

"What did you say?" thundered the Chief Marshal.

"Of course. That's one reason I had to be snatched. The Merchants and Miners Bank. Of course. Of course."

"What evidence?" demanded Fisano.

"None. . . . None. . . ." Craig said. "But that's the place."

"So that's the spot!" Fisano said, as if humoring a child. "So what do we do about it?"

"Why," Craig answered as if explaining the self-evident to a child, "we have a false alarm. We figure out where the fire's apt to be set and we lay for the firebugs. We nab them, of course, and then we turn in the alarm and the apparatus comes. Third alarm. We might even have to have smudge pots to make the illusion perfect. We have to be ready, starting now."

"He's taking charge of the Bureau!" exclaimed the Chief, not without elaborate irony.

Again Nora spoke. She had been so still her presence had passed unnoticed. "You had better heed him," she said. "It could be reason or logic. Or it could be the second sight."

"I am not fey," Craig said shortly. " 'Tis facts and logic. Under cover of the fire they will come. With a police car or a fire department car or some other car that would have natural business there. A car with armed men wearing rubber masks over their faces."

"Go ahead, boy."

"So they will loot the bank and drive away, and no trace will be found of what kind of a car it is."

"Like that robbery of the jewelry store," said Fisano.

"Like that," said Craig eagerly. "And so we have a choice."

"Between what and what?" asked the Chief Marshal.

"Of capturing them in the bank, or of letting them get away with it and capturing them where they hide."

"If we knew where they would hide."

"Oh, we know that, of course. Where the kids' baseball team used to play. Where William Tecumseh Peabody was locked up. Where Clyde Tupper is a prisoner right now."

"Is this more stuff out of that crystal ball?" demanded the Chief Marshal.

"Oh, no, sir," said Craig in a straightforward way. "It's as plain as the nose on your face when you think about it."

"Take it step by step. Grab our little paddies and lead us along as if we were kiddies," said the Chief Marshal in a strangled voice. "And if you're playing smart games with me, me lad, I will tear your tongue from your big mouth with my bare hands."

"There are spaces you have to jump," said Craig with a helpless gesture of his hands. "There are things that aren't coupled up. Where you have to take off and leap."

"And the high muck-a-muck?" demanded the Chief Marshal. "I suppose you have his full name and address?"

Craig shook his head stubbornly. "If I told you, you wouldn't believe me. You would give me the horse laugh, and right then you'd be sure I'd been talking a bag of nonsense about all of it. I've got no evidence for a court, but I've plenty of evidence for myself." Of a sudden his face darkened and set and became blackly stubborn. "Him I shall not name. He belongs to me, and nobody else shall take him. He killed my father and he struck down Uncle Paddy. In all other things I submit to discipline, sir. In all other things I obey orders. But not on this one thing. I will take this man, and I will take him in such a manner that he knows it is I and that

169

I have smashed him and brought him to his bad end. And with that, sir," he said in a voice that was low and pleading, "you will have to be satisfied."

"Blast and damn it, boy," the Chief Marshal said loudly but grimly, "you have proved nothing."

"I know it well," Craig said, "but when you catch them red-handed it will be proof enough." He stared across at Nora, who nodded to him as if encouraging and abetting. "I cannot even prove that the leak in the Bureau is from the lips of Assistant Fire Marshal Luke Priddy. But I know it to be so."

"But the Merchants and Miners Bank," insisted the Chief.

"That brought it to a head. That's why they came after me. Because I saw *him* casing the place, sir. Because I followed him and he must have seen me."

"You followed him. So what did he do?"

"He went into the bank and cashed a check."

"Incriminating!" exclaimed the Chief. "I suppose a million New Yorkers went into banks to cash checks today."

"Chief," said Lieutenant Fisano, "we're in a bind. We know a major crime is planned. We don't know where the blow will fall or when."

"Correct."

"The whole thing of Batts's may be a mare's nest. But it's all we have. We're taking a chance if we act on it, but we're taking a bigger chance if we don't."

"Nevertheless," roared the Chief, "not a move will I make till I'm told the name of this man that Batts says is the head of it all. That's an order, Batts. Name the name or stand suspended. And that's me last word."

Craig hesitated but a moment. "You'll not believe me. It is not to be believed and you will say I've blown my top."

"The name." The Chief's voice was implacable as he pronounced the word. "The name with no more shilly-shallying."

"The name," answered Craig reluctantly, "is Pieter Van Rensselaer."

There was silence. It was a shocked, weighty silence that seemed to be material. Then the Chief Marshal uttered a sound that was a bark. It was a derisive sound, a sound of incredulity. His face was black with rage. "So you'd be making a fool of me!"

"He is the man," Craig said hopelessly.

"Who," asked Lieutenant Fisano, "is this Van Rensselaer?"

"Nobody but the king of the buffs," answered the Chief. "With an honorary gold badge to prove it. Nobody but a pal of every commissioner for twenty years back. Nobody but a friend and relative of mayors and governors. Ye might as well accuse George Washington of bein' Benedict Arnold. The greatest civilian friend the department has ever had. How looney can you get!"

"I knew how you would take it, sir," Craig said heavily.

"And him you accuse of bein' a firebug and a robber, to say nothing of throwin' in a couple of murders."

"He killed my father," Craig said doggedly.

Lieutenant Fisano intervened. "Chief," he said, "at the moment it is not a man's name that matters. Our job is to prevent a crime. Your young man here may be crazy as a coot, but he's offered us the only chance we have. All right. Say he's addled. Say what you want to. But I say we've got to play along. I go farther, Chief. . . . I say any man, no matter how high, can take a tumble. I say a man who spends his life chasing fires is a nut, and you never can tell when a nut will go bad. You're boss of your Bureau, Chief, and you can give orders to go ahead or to lay off. But as for me and the police department we're going ahead. We're laying our bets on this young man. And we're going to play it the way he suggests."

The Chief scowled at Fisano and scowled even more blackly at Craig Batts. "Did I say I would not go along?" he demanded. "Whenever was the fire department behind the police in any matter? Tell me that." He turned upon Craig. "Young Batts," he snarled, "you've stood me on a slippery spot. And may the devil fly away with ye if ye make me land boom on me backside."

"So we are agreed?" asked Fisano.

"The first thing to do," said the Chief, "is to survey the neighborhood. To pick the likeliest building for the fire. Or the likeliest two or three. And fill them so full of your men and my men that nobody can strike a match without being grabbed."

"And men to protect the bank."

"But," Craig said a bit diffidently, "isn't the chief thing to make sure that there is no leak from either department? A leak would spoil it all."

"There will be no leak," the Chief Marshal said, cutting off each word as with the blade of an ax.

"Everything must be set before the bank opens tomorrow," said Fisano. "I'll go to attend to my end of it." He looked at his watch. "We'll meet again in your office at eight."

"I'm leaving with you," the Chief Marshal said. And then to Craig, "You will report in my office at eight." His eyes, red-rimmed from sleeplessness, remained upon the young man's face. Before he turned to the door he spoke again, and then with a half-bewildered shake of his grizzled head. "Damn and blast," he said in a strange, almost awed tone, "if I don't believe that trick mind of yours has hit the ball into the stands with the bases full."

CHAPTER TWENTY-THREE

IT WAS a busy and trying night. A joint board of strategy headed by the Chief Marshal and Lieutenant Fisano planned the intricate campaign with professional attention to every detail. Infinite precautions had been taken to see there should be no leaks. The block in which the Merchants and Miners Bank was located had been scouted, and every building and business in the vicinity had been examined and appraised as possible locations for the expected incendiary fire. Two structures had been selected as most likely: one a six-story building whose floors were occupied by a couple of dozen small manufacturing concerns; the other by a cheap installment furniture company. Both were filled with inflammable merchandise. During the night hours fire marshals and detectives were smuggled into both buildings, and a special detail of firemen was secreted in each with an equipment of smudge pots with which to simulate fires.

Every assistant fire marshal not definitely on the sick list was on duty somewhere through the night. How many men Fisano had on the job, Craig Batts did not know.

At midnight Craig stood in the Chief Marshal's office waiting to perform an unpleasant duty.

"Call him in," directed the Chief grimly, and Craig walked down the hallway to the room occupied by the Manhattan marshals. He motioned to Luke Priddy, who got up and followed to the room of the head of the Bureau of Fire Investigation. Both young men stood before the burly, grizzled man who sat at the desk.

173

"Priddy," he said, and there was more sadness than anger in his small gray eyes, "Batts has charges to bring against you."

Priddy, his usually quizzical face blank, turned his eyes toward Craig and waited.

"I'm sorry, Luke," Craig said. "The specific charge is that you took a certain file from the cabinet and turned it over to Clyde Tupper. You have been informing Tupper of everything that goes on in this Bureau. Specifically you have kept him aware of every movement I have made. There were things he knew that only you and I were aware of, such as my whereabouts at various times. On two occasions you let him know that I would be in Chief Fogarty's apartment so he could time his visits accordingly, and conduct himself so as to throw suspicion on the Chief."

Priddy stood mute. "You visited Tupper's office. At least once I can prove. It was on the day Tupper's rooms were ransacked."

"How can you prove this?" asked the Chief.

"If you will come with me, sir," Craig said, and led the way back to the general room and to Priddy's desk. "Please look how the articles on his desk are arranged."

It was an orderly desk, everything in its place, but there was a pattern to its orderliness. "He always leaves it so," Craig said. "Not on purpose. Automatically. Probably without knowing it. As you, Chief, when you are thinking hard, always reach across your face with your right hand and tug at your left ear. On the center of his blotter there, he makes a fat diamond with his pencils and pens, and inside it an *L* of two matchsticks or something else. Whenever he doodles he makes that figure, a diamond with an *L* inside it."

"Yes?" prompted the Chief.

"That design was on Tupper's blotter," Craig said.

Luke Priddy continued to stand mute. The trio retraced their steps to the Chief Marshal's office.

"He's made out a prima-facie case," said the Chief heavily. "What have you to say?"

Priddy's attitude was one of *sang-froid*. He shrugged and smiled his ironical smile at Craig. "All tied round with a woolen string," he said. "If he hasn't got me tight now he will have—with that infernal trick mind of his. So all right. I leaked to Tupper. I abstracted that file for Tupper. So he could send it to Chief Fogarty."

"Why? Why?" demanded the Chief.

"I couldn't live in the style I wanted on an Assistant Fire Marshal's salary," Priddy said, as if that were sufficient explanation.

"Why did Tupper send that folder to Fogarty?" asked the Chief. "To incriminate him?"

"No," Priddy said. "To set him on the trail."

"What trail?"

"I don't know, but of someone Tupper wanted to do in. Someone who apparently got in first and scragged Tupper."

The Chief Marshal peered curiously at Priddy. "You gave in quick," he said with scorn in his voice. "You put up no fight."

"Well, sir, why wear myself out when I knew I was licked?" the young man said callously.

"Batts," demanded the Chief, "did you find anything else in Tupper's office that you haven't told me about?"

"One thing in particular," Craig said, and drew from his pocket a small envelope from which he shook a triangular bit of glass upon the top of the desk.

"What's that?"

"A fragment of a lens, sir."

"What kind of a lens? Spectacles?"

"No, sir. Not spectacles. A monocle, sir."

"What!"

"Yes, sir. A monocle. I took it to an optician, sir. He said it was a bit of a rimless monocle." Craig paused and stood looking steadily at his superior. "A similar piece of glass," he said, "was found by the examining physician embedded between the second and third knuckles of my father's right hand. . . . And, sir, during the investigation a very important gentleman who attended the fire— permitted that liberty as the king of the buffs—suffered an injury there. It was so noted in his examination. He was struck, so he said, by a falling bit of debris which nearly cut out his right eye. . . . It may mean nothing to you, sir, but to me things equal to the same thing are equal to each other. Why, sir, would my father strike this man with his fist, breaking his eyeglass and lacerating his eye?"

"A little thing," said the Chief to himself.

"But big enough, sir," Craig said soberly.

"You know, Priddy, that Tupper sent this file to Chief Fogarty?"

"I saw it wrapped and addressed and stamped. I mailed it myself."

"You," glowered the Chief, "are suspended, pending formal charges, and may consider yourself under arrest." He became curt. "Batts," he snapped, "call a cop."

The Commissioner came in after midnight, not interfering with the arrangements of police and marshals but listening and watching with keen and intelligent interest. The air was used as little as possible, because the looters and arsonists might, probably did, have radio equipment.

"What about the old brewery?" he asked, as the details of the plan unfolded themselves.

"Mr. Commissioner," said the harried Chief, "tonight we are working on suppositions." His tired, inflamed eyes turned inclemently upon Craig Batts. "No matter how wild-eyed or improbable the suppositions may be, we've got to cover them all."

Craig made a movement as if he would speak but restrained himself in the presence of the Commissioner.

"What is it, young man?" that dignitary asked.

"The brewery, sir," Craig said with unaccustomed diffidence, "fits into the pattern. It's—it's a key piece in the jigsaw puzzle. It keeps bobbing up, sir, from that old boys' baseball team to this moment."

"It seems to do so, young man."

"After the jewelry robbery," Craig went on with more confidence, "the disguised car used by the men in rubber masks disappeared as if erased. The trailer they used for transportation had to be hidden. I've walked the streets, sir, looking for a possible hiding place—into which a car could disappear. And those big doors through which loaded brewery wagons used to come is the most promising place."

"That has, of course, been discussed."

"If," growled the Chief Marshal, "there's going to be a depredation tomorrow, and if the Merchants and Miners Bank is to be the victim; and if there's to be an incendiary fire; and if the criminals are going to make their raid in some kind of a car that would naturally be in such a spot—like a chief's car, or a police prowl car, or some suchlike vehicle, then the old brewery's as good a guess for their headquarters as any."

"And it will be under surveillance?"

"Of course, Commissioner. A fly won't be able to get in or out of it without our knowing. The second those doors open and any kind of a car comes out word will reach us over the air."

The hours dragged. Reports came in by telephone and word of mouth. The speaker at the right of the Chief's desk spluttered and squeaked with routine business, but never a word was carried by the air waves that might be intercepted and betray the presence of the net that was being spread.

Men carrying such a burden found need to talk, to speculate. Taut nerves found some surcease in arguing, in deducing, in pointing out.

"The first word, if any comes," said the Chief, "will be from the firebugs. No firebugs—no raid, and the whole business is a mare's nest."

"The most likely hour," hazarded the Commissioner, "will be just after the opening of the business day."

"It can't come too soon or too early."

It was the uncertainty, the waiting that plucked at their nerves, made them irritable. In the common room down the hall assistant marshals cat-napped with heads on desks. Against the wall in the Chief Marshal's office his aide, chair tilted against the wall, nodded and jerked to wakefulness at any sound. The hours dragged until at last the glow of dawn came through the windows. Canisters of coffee and piles of sandwiches were brought to the floor, and blear-eyed men were grateful for the stimulant. Seven o'clock came. Then watched timepieces announced that it was eight and alertness possessed them all, which, as nine o'clock came around, increased until it became all but unbearable. Any minute now some signal might come, some voice in code over the air or by telephone might give the word that the zero hour had struck and the curtain had arisen upon the melodrama.

As the hands of watches showed the half hour tension reached a point where it seemed that something must crack; that human nerves could be stretched no farther.

177

"And then, at ten minutes before the hour of ten, the telephone jangled and the Chief snatched it from its cradle.

"Chief Marshal speaking," he said harshly into the instrument.

"Got 'em," came back a voice. "One on third floor, one on fifth. Furniture store. Some kind of incendiary bombs."

"Any disturbance to tip off the capture?"

"Not to speak of. Smudge pots going now. Smoke pouring from windows. Alarm turned in."

Over the telephone could now be heard the screech of sirens, and apparatus careened through the streets to the scene of the fire. Then, from the grid of the loud-speaker came another voice. No need for precaution now. The die was cast. The curtain was up and the play was under way.

"Brewery doors opened at 9:51," said the voice. "Telephone service car came out. Four men aboard. Swung south at corner."

From then to the end the battle between the lawless and the guardians of the law was waged to its planned conclusion. On both sides was split-second timing. The false telephone service wagon rolled to a stop before the bank. Four men with strange, unnatural faces leaped to the sidewalk and marched with military precision through the great doors of the financial institution. No hand was raised against them until they committed the overt act, the incriminating act; until they produced weapons and made the demand calculated to cow into submission the tellers of the bank.

Then the concealed men of the police and Fire Marshal's department appeared like magic from their ambush, blocking the way of escape. From behind counters, in the gallery above, appeared men armed with riot guns, with machine guns, with such other weapons as the day and hour demanded.

Not a shot was fired. The odds were too overwhelming for even desperate men to face or to attempt to breast. Weapons dropped to the marble floor; hands reached for the sky. The officers converged upon the four men in rubber masks, and with efficient speed each of the four was adorned with steel bracelets not designed to enhance his beauty.

Commissioner and Chief and those in the office listened with relaxed nerves as report after report crackled in. Stomach muscles softened. Craig was conscious of sudden nausea.

Last report to come was from the brewery, where the house trailer was found and the car with the hitch to draw it.

"We got a man here," said the reporting voice. "Gagged. Hands and feet tied. In a bad way. Send ambulance."

"That," said Craig more to himself than to the others, "will be Clyde Tupper."

"And that," said the Commissioner wearily, "is that."

"Bagged the whole kit and b'lin' of them," echoed the Chief Marshal.

"Not all," Craig contradicted grimly.

"All but who?" snarled the Chief.

"All," said Craig, "but the head man. All but the one we need most to get. All but Pieter Van Rensselaer." The young man spoke with quiet savagery. "All," he went on and not without grim irony, "but the king of the buffs."

CHAPTER TWENTY-FOUR

IT HAD been, as final reports came in, a complete roundup of the arson ring with the one exception of the man who planned and led its depredations. More than one person in high official or social positions would be appalled to learn that the impeccable Pieter Van Rensselaer, scion of one of New York's historic families, was the master mind of a criminal organization. It might even be that powerful influences would rally around him to avert altogether or to minimize his punishment. But murder is a misdeed which even the most potent intervention finds it difficult to minimize.

"The man must be insane," said the Commissioner.

"William Tecumseh Peabody thought so, sir," said Craig Batts.

"But cunningly insane," said the Chief Marshal.

"After many, many years of leading so successful a double life he must have come to believe himself to be untouchable," the Commissioner said. "He must have added megalomania to his other mental quirks. Illusions of grandeur. Belief in his all-powerfulness; his superiority to all other men."

"Giving all laws the horse laugh," said the Chief Marshal. "He certainly had us all bamboozled."

"May I suggest," said Craig, "that this thing that has happened today will be a terrific shock to his unstable mind? It may send him completely off his rocker, so that there will be no predicting what he may do."

"He's a conspicuous person," said the Commissioner. "With all the police force and all the men of this Bureau searching for him, he won't be able long to remain at large."

Craig was thinking to himself that Van Rensselaer might not try to hide. He might try to evade for a time. But his mania might concentrate into singleness of purpose. His megalomania might be unable to tolerate that he had been outthought, outmaneuvered, utterly defeated. The man's mind had been keen and efficient in its insane workings—abnormally brilliant. Otherwise it would not have been able to plan so successfully or to lead with such astounding success a double life.

His attempt to kidnap Craig was sure evidence that he had been watching the young man, was aware that Craig was becoming a danger to him. Now, in this moment of complete debacle, he would realize that it was chiefly through the determination and skill and peculiar mentality of the youthful assistant fire marshal that he had come to his Waterloo.

Would not, then, all his rancor, his venom, his frustration and his insane rage settle itself upon Craig Batts? Would he not believe that he was required to revenge himself upon the man who had cast him down from his high estate? Would he not, at no matter what cost to himself, wreak vengeance upon the man he regarded as his prime enemy and destroyer?

Craig guessed, not wholly without justification, that this would be so. And, with a touch of extrasensory perception, he reached a conviction that Pieter Van Rensselaer would not be taken by police or marshals until he had made his try. With a queer exaltation he came to know, or to think he knew, that in the end it would be between Van Rensselaer and himself. Between the son of a murdered father and the man who had committed that murder.

He became conscious that the Chief Marshal was eying him sharply.

"Assistant Marshal Batts," he said with weary formality, "you look as if you were about to cave in. I feel as if I were about to cave in. When men reach the breaking point there's no remedy but sleep. . . . Your case will be taken up in due time by the Commissioner and myself. Meantime we shall all be the better for six hours' sleep." He looked at his watch. It was, incredible as it seemed to all of them, but one o'clock in the afternoon.

"Report here at seven-thirty," he said.

With dragging feet they walked to the elevator and descended to the street. On the subway carrying him to Brooklyn, Craig rode between sleep and waking; he nodded and jerked erect; lost consciousness for a moment and then snapped awake. At last he reached his destination and all but staggered the few blocks to his apartment, where, strewing his clothing about the floor, he fell upon his bed and was instantly asleep.

It seemed but a minute before he was disturbed by the insistent ringing of the telephone bell. So deep was he in sleep that it was not easy to climb out of that abyss to awareness. Resentfully he lifted the instrument and put it to his ear.

"Hello," he mumbled.

"Would this," inquired an oleaginous voice, "be Assistant Fire Marshal Batts?"

"Yes," snapped Batts. "What's wanted?"

"This, if you will overlook my, shall we say brashness, in interrupting your siesta, is Soapy Japes."

"And what the devil do you want, Soapy?"

"Sir," Soapy said, "I know my place. I know it is an imposition to make this request of you. But, sir, it is of the first importance. There is an individual, sir, of whom you desire information. A friend and companion of my late employer. If, Mr. Batts, you will come here with all possible celerity I will be able to put you in touch with that individual. I say this with all certainty, sir. I would say it to you. I would say it to the Commissioner of the fire department. I would tell it to the Marines."

Craig held the instrument glued to his ear for an interval. Then he spoke into the receiver. "I'm on my way," he said.

He was wide awake. With the efficiency of the trained fireman he dressed himself, repeating over and over Soapy's final words. "I would say it to you. I would say it to the Commissioner of the fire department. I would tell it to the Marines."

Adroit old confidence man! Skillful user of words to deceive. Soapy Japes with one phrase had delivered his message. "Tell it to the Marines." With those words he had told it to Craig, told him that the telephone message had been sent under duress! Told him that Soapy had delivered his message with a gun against his ribs. The little, preternaturally sober-faced, courageous ex-sharper had taken his life in his hands to transmit a warning.

So Pieter Van Rensselaer was in William Tecumseh Peabody's house! He was waiting there for Craig Batts to walk into his parlor. It was an invitation to the finale. An invitation to an inevitable, predestined meeting.

Craig might have armed himself but he did not do so. Without doubt Pieter Van Rensselaer would have provided himself with firearms. But Craig did not want to kill the man. He did not want o cope with that temptation. His burning desire was to take the man alive, and alive to deliver him up to the law for punishment.

His head was clear of sleep. Physically he felt as fit as he had ever done in his athletic life. And his mental state was one of optimism, almost of gaiety as he went to this rendezvous. He whistled tunelessly.

It was his duty to have notified headquarters, but he would not do that, because what was imminent was between himself alone and Van Rensselaer. The subway train seemed to crawl, but at last it reached his station. Craig mounted to the street. Then with resolute strides he walked to the Peabody residence and descended to the area door. Precautions would be useless. Any attempt to effect a secret entrance would be futile. He did not consider it. His thumb pressed the bell. The first instant would be the one of prime peril. If Van Rensselaer did not shoot at once, then the first hurdle would have been surmounted. Craig did not believe the man would shoot at once. He believed his enemy would give way to the urge to talk; to preen himself; to jeer at his enemy. He would not be contented with a quick killing, but his twisted mind would require that it be embellished with words.

The door swung inward and Soapy Japes stood revealed, pale, eyes staring.

"You—you came anyway," he stammered.

"But thanks, Soapy. I came anyway."

"Step in, my friend," said Van Rensselaer from behind Soapy. "Step into my parlor."

It was Van Rensselaer's voice but it was not Van Rensselaer's face. The world had suddenly gone fantastic, unreal, zany, for the man was wearing a rubber mask that made his face look as if made from wax and had no relation to anything human.

Craig stepped past Soapy, and Van Rensselaer gave back a step.

"Follow me, please," he said in a voice somewhat muffled by the rubber. He giggled. "I know how to make men do my bidding," he said. "I plan. I concoct. I direct. I impose my will." He motioned down the hall with his automatic, allowing Craig to pass him in the narrow way, and then thrusting the muzzle of his gun against Craig's ribs.

They mounted to the kitchen, and Van Rensselaer prodded Craig through that room toward the front of the house and into William Tecumseh Peabody's fine library, which was adequately lighted.

"Come here, Mr. Batts," Van Rensselaer ordered. "I will occupy this seat behind my old friend's desk. You stand there in front with both hands flat on the blotter. Now step back a pace. Like that. A very helpless position indeed. . . . You, Soapy, stand there with your nose against the wall. . . . Excellent."

"Why do you wear that mask?" Craig asked. "Not to conceal your identity."

"Oh, no. I wear it in an antic mood."

"I shouldn't think you would feel very antic, Mr. Van Rensselaer."

"Was Napoleon in despair when he was sent to Elba?"

"It didn't tickle him to death," Craig said.

"It was a mere setback."

"But then," Craig said, "came Waterloo."

"I," said Van Rensselaer, "would have managed better. I shall manage better now. I wouldn't have come to this had it not been for you, Mr. Batts. I shall start over again, but there will be no you to meddle."

Craig fanned the man's vanity with flattery. "For years you fooled everybody. You were wonderful."

"They even gave me a gold badge. The king of the buffs. I diddled them all. I'll diddle them all again."

"I suppose you had a good reason for everything you did? You won't want people to think you did foolish things."

"I did no foolish things. Everything had its reason. Some that seemed unwise were forced upon me by necessity."

"Like, for instance, killing my father?"

"His own fault. In those days I hadn't a perfect organization. I had to do things myself. Your father detected me in the act of doing a thing. He struck me, and naturally I had to shoot him."

"Oh, naturally," Craig said. "And, of course, you had to kill William Tecumseh Peabody?"

"He brought it on himself. My good friend. Do you know we were on the same ball team years ago? But he was eccentric, Mr. Batts. He fancied himself as a Haroun-al-Raschid, prowling the streets of Bagdad at night. He prowled too much. It was not so much what he found out that made his removal necessary. It was his supreme insult to me. Fancy, Mr. Batts! He dared to doubt my sanity." He shrugged his perfectly tailored shoulders. "I am averse to killing people, so I merely removed him; to a place you know of

But he escaped and was going to—'blab' is the *mot juste* to another old friend and teammate."

"Chief Fogarty?"

"Of whom I was very fond. Indeed I became in some measure his benefactor. A splendid man, sir. Splendid. Of impregnable integrity. But financially a babe in arms. So, because of my great affection, I handled for him his inventions."

"Inventions?"

"To be sure. The Eureka Air Pack for one. A very superior mask, patented and moderately profitable. And a beautiful improvement to the fog nozzle. And other gadgets. These made some thousands of dollars for him."

"But those thousands of dollars on deposit might have been misconstrued."

"No indeed. The Commissioner was aware of every stage of the transaction. No obloquy could possibly attach."

"But this man Clyde Tupper was trying to blackmail him."

Van Rensselaer giggled again. "Paddy Fogarty was putting it on his eye," he said gleefully. "Setting traps. . . . Until Tupper cast aspersions upon myself. Then Paddy was sorely troubled."

"You make it all very clear," Craig said. "They won't be able to keep a good man down. . . . That should be shouted from the housetops." He ventured to turn his eyes toward Soapy Japes. "Somebody should shout for you. Somebody should scream it at the top of his voice."

Craig, during the colloquy, had edged first one foot and then the other closer to the heavy, ornate desk. He wondered painfully if Soapy would understand his demand, or would have courage to obey it. But he had but an instant of doubt. From Soapy's throat came a screech, weird, startling, ululating, the agony of one in torture.

Van Rensselaer's eyes jerked away from Craig. He was startled, frightened, half paralyzed by the sudden eeriness of it. And in that instant Craig's hands darted to the edge of the desk and he heaved with all his strength. Desk and chair and Pieter Van Rensselaer toppled to the floor with a crash. The man's legs were imprisoned under the heavy piece of furniture, his back was wrenched as it collided with the chair, and his head collided sickeningly with the floor. Like a high diver Craig lunged across the tangle and fastened upon Van Rensselaer's throat. Almost at the same instant the alert

Soapy snatched the automatic from where it had fallen to the rug.

But there was no need for further violent action. Van Rensselaer was stunned, *hors de combat*. Craig, as though by sleight of hand, produced steel handcuffs from his pocket and snapped them on the dapper aristocrat's wrists, and then ungently hauled him to his feet, where he stood, head swaying and grotesque with its mask of rubber.

"This time," Craig said grimly, "Waterloo came bloody quickly after the landing from Elba."

He thrust Van Rensselaer into an overstuffed chair, where the man slumped, near to unconsciousness. Then he picked up the telephone which had been cast to the floor and dialed headquarters. He was panting, and weariness had returned to sit heavily upon him.

"Assistant Marshal Batts here," he said. "Telephone the Chief. I've got handcuffs on Pieter Van Rensselaer. . . . In William Tecumseh Peabody's library. . . . Somebody better come get him —before I—black out."

He hung up the receiver and then dialed again. This time he was calling Uncle Paddy Fogarty's apartment. It was Nora who answered.

"Darlin'," he said and then repeated, "darlin'. The game's over, honey. The other team got no runs and no hits. Uncle Paddy in the clear, and never was anywhere else. As we both knew. . . . As to you and me, personally, Pumpkin Pie, I stand in need of food and refreshment."

"It will be waiting for you," Nora said.

"And," he said, and the brogue sounded sweet in her ears, "whin I have et and drunk, thin br-race yoursilf, for then comes the wooin' and the courtin' to make all others' efforts alongst that line seem pale an' puny."

"My dear," she replied, and her voice was grave but also very joyous, "what happens when the irresistible wooing collides with the immovable everlastin' love?"

"There befalls a thing," he said softly, "that set the Little People to caperin' ring around rosy." He paused a moment and said his final word. "But fir-r-rst comes a steak smothered in ounions, and mashed praties and steamin' coffee wit' vegetables on the side and pie to follow. . . . I'll be there, my dear, before they've stopped sizzlin' in the pan."

Where
There's
Smoke

NOVELS BY CLARENCE BUDINGTON KELLAND

Where There's Smoke
West of the Law
The Case of the Nameless Corpse
Death Keeps a Secret
Murder Makes an Entrance
Dangerous Angel
Tombstone
The Key Man
The Great Mail Robbery
Stolen Goods
This Is My Son
Merchant of Valor
Double Treasure
Land of the Torreones
Alias Jane Smith
Heart on Her Sleeve
Archibald the Great
Sugarfoot
Silver Spoon
Valley of the Sun
Scattergood Baines Returns
Arizona
Skin Deep
Star Rising
Spotlight
The Forgotten Man
Roxana

Dreamland
Jealous House
The Cat's Paw
The Great Crooner
Speak Easily
Gold
Hard Money
Dynasty
Knuckles
Sudden Jim
The Source
The Little Moment of Happiness
The High Flyers
The Hidden Spring
Efficiency Edgar
Thirty Pieces of Silver
Youth Challenges
Scattergood Baines Pulls the Strings
Scattergood Baines
Contraband
Conflict
The Steadfast Heart
Miracle
Rhoda Fair
Dance Magic